The South Side

The South Side
Three Glasgow Novellas

Moira Burgess

Kennedy & Boyd
an imprint of
Zeticula
57 St Vincent Crescent
Glasgow
G3 8NQ
Scotland

http://www.kennedyandboyd.co.uk
admin@kennedyandboyd.co.uk

Copyright © Moira Burgess 2011
Cover photograph © Kenny Whyte 2011

ISBN-13 978-1-84921-084-3

Contents

Below

1

She lay warm and more than half asleep in the kitchen bed and heard footsteps going about. The waking fire purred and cracked. Water ran into the kettle, constantly changing its song. The radio was quietly on. She couldn't see them, but ' – ready?' her father said, and her mother murmured, and the hot smell of porridge rose, and the cold smell of milk. 'Still sleeping,' her mother said. 'Let her sleep.'

But they stripped back the hard clean sheet and slapped lukewarm water on her belly and thighs. They wouldn't let her sleep and they couldn't get her clean. 'You'll never get that off,' she wanted to say, but she couldn't seem to speak.

'Naw, you'll have to dae that yersel,' Pat Brady said, though he wasn't there. Wouldn't let him over the door, him and his smelly dog. 'Kuwait?' she said. 'Who would call a dog Kuwait?'

'Fancied the sound o it,' Brady said. 'An see, he likes it, he's waggin his fuckin tail.'

They were flopping her over and back, tossing her from hand to hand. One was gentle and one was brusque but she didn't like either of them. 'Are you ready?' Cameron barked, and she said 'I don't know. How the fuck am I supposed to know?'

Naw, I never said that. A wee librarian lassie like me?

They were handling her like a pillow and she much preferred to be in charge. 'Tell you what,' she said to Cameron, 'let's try it this way,' but he wasn't happy with that way, not at all. Flat on his back, a fixed smile, joy of sex, forget it. 'Oh, all right,' she said, and rolled off, and lay down.

Gentle, on the other hand? Never had the chance.

'What's your name, love?' somebody said. She wasn't able to reply. 'Down by the –' people were saying. 'Under the – Found her beside – Not sure if she –'

'Do we know who she is?' said the soft Irish voice, warm as porridge and cream.

'The state she was in,' said the hard one, 'I don't suppose she knows herself.'

Knows herself, the tall white room echoed back. High ceiling. That's good. No problem in the kitchen bed. But under the bed. And another day.

'Ah, you wouldn't want to let Mr Dinnet hear you saying that,' murmured the gentle voice.

'It's well and very well for Mr Dinnet,' the hard young north voice said. 'He doesn't have to clean them up.'

'Nurse! Nurse!' called Mr Dinnet, far away. He didn't like to have to say it twice. Well, obviously he did, because once would have been quite enough. The gentle nurse went skittering off in a panic as if he might be going to skelp her arse for her. The hard one pulled up the stiff white sheet and tucked it in by numbers, one, two, three.

Ah, they can make mistakes too, Belle wanted to say to the gentle nurse. The surgeon came swaggering in through the swing doors and peacocked there in his frock coat and tile hat. Sideboards combed fluffy, thumbs in his oxters. No need for an operation here, sister! Give the fellow an aspirin and send him home! And the young guy with the brain tumour jumped off the suspension bridge on the way home. And Sir William the brain surgeon walks the hospital corridors to this day. Serve him fuckin well right.

Can't see what's under their fuckin noses. 'Pull yourself together, Agnes,' her father said.

The ward went quiet and Belle was lying in bed. In a bed. Funny that. Belle, that's who I am.

That's who I am?

In the opposite bed was a woman but it wasn't her mother, who'd never made it this far. Other women to right and left. How can I see them, when I'm lying flat and so are they?

Not lying flat but floating free. Belle could see the whole ward, a mile long and more, two straight rows of beds marching into a pearly mist where white figures huddled by a great glass door. 'It was for the best,' somebody said. Not to Belle.

Above each bed was a high window reaching to the sky. Belle, floating, looked out. 'What a fuckin mess,' she said, and so it was, the old city, jumbled with red tenements and glass offices, gap sites, swooping motorways, bridges, walkways, stairs. Fireworks were going off because it was Hogmanay or Diwali or the millennium or some fuckin thing. She saw a canyon of a street threading through the rubble, through the clanging noise. Something very deep at its end.

She stood at the heavy swing doors of the ward. CLEMENT ATTLEE WARD, it was called. Funny that.

'Go away, Patrick,' she said. 'Naethin to dae wi you.'

'Sure aboot that, are you?' Pat Brady enquired.

'Are you ready?' That wasn't Brady. Not even Cameron. Maybe herself.

'How the fuck am I supposed to know?'

She was alone. She was riding a steep escalator which ought to be going up but instead was going down. Faces glimmered on the painted walls, distorted, out of true. Until you were level with them, eye to eye, and then you wished them skew again.

'All men,' she pointed out chattily to Cameron. Naturally he hadn't noticed that.

'They couldn't think of a famous woman!' he brayed. 'I wonder why!'

'What about me?'

Cameron laughed. The doctor laughed. Kuwait the dog sat back on his hindquarters and panted with glee. It was very clear to see that he hadn't had his trip to the vet, any more than the dogs before him, Kabul or Derry or Saigon or Yang. Cameron had all the equipment too, though you'd wonder sometimes in the panting sad night.

'Costs money,' Pat Brady said, and he was taller than her, and she was a strapping big girl. His hair was black and rough because barbers cost money too.

'Besides which,' said Belle. She stepped off the escalator and shouldered past the surgeon's ghost and barged through another set of swing doors.

Fierce red winter sunrise making the broken glass on the wasteground wink scarlet and gold. Hard frost overnight and snow to come. So what fuckin else is new? She wrung out a cloth under the standpipe and began to sponge her neck, her tangled oxters, the sweaty channels under her breasts. The raw wind off the river scoured her goosepimpled skin. 'That okay for youse?' she yelled to the TV crew.

'Just finish it off for us, Belle, there's a love.'

On a monitor stuck up on the fence she could see the opening credits, though they wouldn't get to that stage for months. 'Working title only,' the director assured her. *Chronicles of a Bag Lady* was the best they'd come up with so far.

'But that's no who I am.'

'Oh, sorry, Belle, love, thought it was.'

Inch by inch with the dawn-cold washcloth over her skinny belly and thighs. Behind, between. 'Thought you said I'd be able to get it aff,' she complained.

'No yet,' Pat Brady said.

'Yah, thanks, Belle, that's excellent, we got a good effect with the light there.'

She put on her stockings, buttoned her skirt, zipped her boots, as the sun wheeled behind the tilting tower blocks. Camera tricks. She knotted her flaming orange silk headscarf under her chin and pulled her raincoat belt tight. One and a half times round her waist. 'Have to fatten you up,' Cameron said, clapping her on the bum.

'What we want to know, Belle, is how you got here.'

She sat on the top of a hill as the cold light left the sky. Navy-blue clouds climbed out of the north behind the multicoloured high flats. Down among her plastic bags there was a rustle and a click of teeth. She kicked her booted heel against the bench and the sharp feet scuttered away.

'The light's going, Belle,' they complained, 'this isn't going to work.'

'I'm lookin for somethin,' she said.

'What would that be, Belle?'

'If I fuckin knew I wouldny be fuckin lookin,' she said. 'Gonny stop callin me Belle every fuckin breath you draw?'

'That's who you are, isn't it?' the director said.

She hauled the food bag up on to her lap and found the jaggy rip where green teeth had got through. Past the bare flower beds at the edge of the pond she could see a big new plastic bag crumpled in a bin.

'Aye but it's no that simple,' she said. 'See if I go an get it? Come back and where's ma fuckin bags? It's happened afore now,' she told the TV crew. They got busy and filmed it happening, the bags getting whisked up, raked through, chucked into the pond.

As she hooked the new bag on to a bent finger she heard the last evening sound: clang, clang, clang, clang, far away on all four sides, the parkies shutting the gates. Though you didn't get parkies now. 'They're supposed to check,' she said. 'Dae they check? Dae they fuck. I could be dead on that bench and they'd let me lie.' The cameraman filmed a blackbird chittering at her under a bush. Its deep soft feathers were the colour Patrick Brady's hair used to be, but it looked at her with a cold park-keeper's eye.

She found the place where the railings were wrenched apart. Incredible Hulk wuz here. Stiff as an old horse she clambered through, and the TV crew were on the other side already, filming her. Under the heavy sky she came to a street she knew. What used to be a street. Gawky high flats squared their courtyards around it, but one block of weeds and rubble was still there. One solitary tenement on its edge. Belle stared at the lit window three stairs up. Somebody was crying. 'Can I go up there?' she said.

'Oh, we've got a lot to do before that,' the director said. The soundman checked his levels, tuning out the crying and the panting sobs.

'A constant process of demolition,' the voice-over man said, though he wasn't going to be dubbed in for weeks yet. 'Knock down the tenements, build high flats. Knock down the flats, build a shopping mall.'

'But what we're saying, love, is that it's all still there.'

'Still there?'

'Still there.' Dipping, zooming, grainy black-and-white archive shots. The portico of a church. Old painted lettering above a shop door. A stream choked with rubbish, oozing under a bridge. 'Layers, could we say?' the director said.

'There's a whole street under the Central Station.' That was Cameron putting his oar in. The director leafed through the notes on her clipboard, a bit annoyed. 'Built over and it's still there,' Cameron was saying through his pipe-stem. 'Cobbles, pavements, houses, shops, all still there.'

'Wouldn't the trains fall through?' Belle said. Cameron wasn't very pleased.

'This we must see!' the director cried.

'It's how to find it,' objected Belle. 'It's no very easy to find.' She started out across town. The sun rose again, because the director wanted it to.

'Maybe that's what you're looking for, Belle,' they eagerly said. And they started to run. All the way from the park to the golden ship on the steeple, to the poem in the middle of the river, to the graves of the tobacco lords, to the lost village, wherever the fuck that might be.

Crowds in the water-meadow of the willow trees, packed elbow to elbow so that you couldn't get through. Belle walked along the street on the tops of their heads. 'I didn't know you could do this sort of thing here,' panted the director at her back.

'You don't know much, dae ye?' said Belle.

The mic flex got looped round someone's neck. 'Watch it, dickhead,' advised the cameraman as the body bumped and swung above the crowd.

'Don't tell her,' said the voice-over man behind Belle's back.

'Course not.'

'She doesn't need to know.'

Belle turned round, but everything had been cleared away. A coffin was being passed over the heads of the crowd, hand to hand. 'Get a grip, Belle,' they all said.

'I want you to see this,' announced Cameron, stopping in the middle of the street and bringing the whole procession to a halt, bang, bang, bang into each other's backs like Laurel and Hardy. 'A bank. There's something safe about a bank.' Pat Brady and the dog Kuwait stood in the street outside but nobody would let them in.

'It's shut, ya wanker,' said Belle. 'Look at the gates.'

'Yes, *look* at the gates! Old pennies!' trilled the director, and the camera zoomed into a close-up. The handles of the doors were bronze pennies bigger than Cameron's head, and that was big. You only saw them when the door was shut, when you couldn't get in. Cameron smoked his pipe and said 'No career for a woman in banking, dear.'

'Even Cameron knows better by this time,' said the director doubtfully.

'Could be Cameron's dad,' said Belle. 'Like faither like son. Could be my faither come to that.' Cameron slapped her bum and said 'When we have a boy he'll be another Cameron, of course.' A black-haired lanky young guy passed the end of the street. 'His eyes are too close together,' pointed out Cameron. 'Catholics, you can always tell.'

'We must get the Art School,' insisted the director. The street blossomed into Mackintosh roses. 'It was his wife that designed them,' observed Belle, batting them away, but Cameron didn't hear her, nodding wisely and remarking 'Cultural industries' round his pipe-stem. They stood looking up at a cliff-wall with windows where you wouldn't expect windows to be.

'Get this,' the director said to the cameraman. 'It's the south elevation and we can't see it now.'

'So how the fuck can you film it?' objected Belle.

'It's *there*,' the director said patiently, 'we just can't see it,' sounding very like Cameron, and sure enough here came Cameron with news of this guy who knew somebody who'd take them down to see the buried village when his pal could get the key.

'Well, I'd fuckin hope so,' said Belle. 'I've been lookin for it long enough.'

'That's no whit you're lookin for, Belle,' Pat Brady said.

They passed the Duke of Wellington's statue, beaky and high on his horse, and she certainly wasn't looking for that. 'My lord returned from the wars today and did pleasure me in his top-boots,' a distant voice said, though it might have been a different duke. He had a traffic-cone on his head and so had his horse. They were in George Square among another slew of statues. 'In this whole town there's only three statues of women,' Belle said. Camera angles swooped and dipped so that you saw bits you didn't usually see, but still not even an ankle under Queen Victoria's skirts, sidesaddle on her pacing horse.

'Better check that,' the director said, making a note.

'What about this lot?' the cameraman objected, and across the façade of the City Chambers he ran a montage of sculptured women draped in flowing robes. Partly draped. 'Aye, well,' said Belle, 'that's Industry wi her tits oot, she'll need tae watch she disny catch them in the rollers, an that's a Nubian slave, they've let her keep her turban on. I'll dae ye a statue o a real wumman,' and she danced on an empty plinth with her raincoat and her orange scarf flapping in the breeze. The camera veered to look up her skirt.

'We need to know how you got there, Belle.'

'Ask Cameron.' He climbed up on the plinth and tried some of his kinky stuff, backside foremost and over his knee, but Belle punched him out and there was still the one way he wouldn't try. The cameraman ran out of film.

'Get a grip, love, we've still got Rabbie to do. Says here he's holding a wee sleekit timorous daisy?' The statue gazing poetically at its upraised hand. 'Can you see it, Belle?'

'Some cunt's nicked it again.'

And they were racing up the High Street in the teeth of a half-gale. Brady lurched out from among the lashing trees on the top of the hill, stinking like a brewery. Kuwait snapped at the director's legs. 'Jesus, how did the wino get into shot?' the cameraman said.

'Nasty piece of work. Eyes too close together. Born to be hung,' said Cameron, or maybe Cameron's dad. Or Belle's father, come to that.

'Where's Belle? What's the matter with Belle?' they said, and the director explained: 'It's you we're interested in, Belle.'

'Get a load of this then,' said Belle, 'twice nightly, seats in all parts,' and under King Billy's statue she rolled with Brady on the short-mown grass. She hauled her drawers off and flung them away, nearly hitting the cameraman in the eye. Sparse hair rubbed her and she could feel how stringy and dry Patrick's bare legs were. Likely so were her own. 'Ah God, Pat, we wasted a lot of time,' she said. Rose smiled at them, because Rose was dead.

'There's something we want to show you, Belle,' they said.

They were standing in the street, the whole crew, ranged in a line along a bit of wall which most of them were too short to see over. No problem for Belle, who was floating in mid-air. Tin cans and toilet paper with a dribble of black water oozing between. The director got really excited. The cameraman nearly sprained his wrist keeping up with her demands. The voice-over man intoned it like an anthem: 'All that can now be seen of the Molendinar Burn.'

'Layers. It's still there,' the director breathed.

'It's a fuckin drain,' said Belle. 'Honks like one too.'

'The oldest, deepest place,' the voice-over man said. 'Where the ox-cart stopped. Where Kentigern built his church. Where it all began. And it's still there.'

'It's fuckin filthy.'

'It is now.'

'Youse are tryin to tell me somethin,' Belle complained.

They were in the Merchant City and Cameron was quite at home, strutting between the sheer warehouse walls. 'Wake up an smell the tobacco,' said Belle, and it was Cameron's pipe or maybe her father's full-strength Craven A. 'Very cold,' the director noted in some excitement, and the voice-over man chimed in: 'Round every corner we expect to see the ghost of a tobacco lord –'

'That's no why it's cold,' said Belle. Nobody could hear the weeping but herself.

'Are we looking for the old village? Is it anywhere near here?'

Down in the Trongate night was coming on and there was singing in the music hall, and a lot of jokes Cameron wouldn't understand. Through the cobbled closes and in the courtyards you could hear guys and lassies scuffling and squealing, and there was a ghost pissing in the corner of a dim-lit pend. He looked over his shoulder and it was Pat Brady grinning with gappy teeth. 'Sure me and Belle's pals from way back,' he said. 'I can take yez there.'

He led them off the map into a net of courtyards and lanes. Smoky steam caught at their throats under the high glass canopy where you could fancy already you smelled the sea. They came to a blank wall with thirty years of moss where there used to be a door. 12/6 Return, said a freckle of yellow paper stuck to the stone.

'Cheap at the price,' said Belle.

'Naw, this is right, we'll find it here.' But in the crooked lane with broken buildings above they lost their way. They had even lost the station, though it was there somewhere, they could feel it overhead, like a great foundered ship in the sky. Slimy green walls brushing their shoulders, shattered slates clinking under their feet. They stood in a square littered courtyard with the empty eyes of barred windows looking down. Through an archway they could see a pedimented door, but when they looked again it wasn't there. Above them, under a sodium sky, the high bridge carried its bright beetles of cars, running, running on.

'Canny be far away,' said Brady. 'I know a guy that knows a guy that knows a guy that's got a key.'

'Promises, promises,' said Belle.

'The thing is, Belle, we don't know where it is,' the director said.

'We're waiting for you to tell us,' said the voice-over man.

'Show us the way,' said the cameraman. 'Take us there.'

'It's no near here. It's naethin but money here. Aye was. Is again.'

'Yes,' said the director, 'we need to set that scene. Glass skyscrapers. Offces. Restaurants. Wine bars.' And as she named them, up they sprang like a pop-up book, unfolding, extending, arrowing into the sky. You couldn't see where the Molendinar was, or where the old village might be.

There was a door at the end of the street. Not a door, just the frame of a door, with the cold dawn wind blowing both round and through.

2

Even though they'd filmed the washing scene already, Belle washed herself fiercely, scrupulously, every inch, under the tall glass office blocks that caught fire from the rising sun. Thin shoulders and skinny breasts and the tender nape of her neck where the dirt seemed to stick. Head under the standpipe to work up a carbolic lather in her short straight bottlebrush hair that used to be as red as the sunrise sky. 'Every fuckin morning in life,' she said when the director tried to point out that they'd done it before. 'No gonny change ma routine for youse.' And huffily they drew back to the edge of the wasteground to do fly-on-the-wall. Supposing there'd been a wall.

Anyway she could see like a TV camera herself, could see everywhere, even up her own arse, because she was now-Belle watching then-Belle strip-washing on the wasteground in a spring dawn. 'Gonny be stuff they wouldny even show on Five,' she said. She thought she heard the cameraman chuckle. Definitely it was the director who said 'Yah, well, there you have it, cleanest bag-lady in town.'

'Yez needny think I wis always a bag-lady,' she said.

But everybody had heard it before and anyway they were still asleep. Tam Ratface was wheezing in his corner, sorry for himself and well he might be. Skinny Lizzie was so flat she was nearly not there. Sometimes you'd see two pairs of feet sticking out below her Indian blanket. Usually nobody was that desperate, not by a long, long way. Pat Brady was spark out. He'd finished the Buckie. Tenderly brewed by monks. Not what you'd call a regular communicant thae days but at least he shows his support.

That's why she got up early, so she could wash all over and nobody would see. Those blazing towers were on the other side of the motorway, the other side of the world, no danger there. On the wasteground behind her a broken warehouse window glinted back the watery light and she smelt spring in the damp stone. Fuckin spring. Her hipbones creaked with pain she could nearly hear. She pulled on her knickers, fastened her skirt.

'Ya missed a bit,' croaked Pat Brady from under his coats.

'Aw Jesus,' she said, 'it's alive.' He ground his knuckles into his sticky eye-sockets and blinked at her, black coal eyes in a grey ash face. In among the white stubble on his chin there was egg yolk from fuck knows when. 'Never could haud it,' said now-Belle, though in fact she'd seen him worse.

Lizzie poked her pencil nose out of the blanket. 'Which bit, Patrick?' slavering worse than Kuwait. It's no that she wants tae know. Wants tae hear him say it. Cameron in the night.

'Naethin he hasny seen afore.' I wish. ('I wish? Where on earth did you pick that up?' Cameron sighed.) 'Gonny have a bath yersel, Patrick, it wouldny kill you?'

'It's no very easy,' groaned Brady.

'I'll gie you a hand.' That was Lizzie of course.

'Fuckin lea me in peace,' and he pulled the coats over his head.

One coat was his own and one he'd found. He had a blanket roll but it was solid with damp, stinking with mould. Passing, she ran her thumbnail through its greenish iridescent bloom, and moved it farther away from his hunched back that juddered to his difficult breaths. Kuwait the dog opened an eye and twitched an ear. 'His cough's bad enough already,' Belle explained, and Kuwait went back to sleep.

People were waking. You could smell the little smoky smudge-fires kindling and smouldering and beginning to lick flame. The particular cold striking up from the dawn river sliced into her back and she felt her kidneys twinge. The mud-flats beneath the embankment flickered with running rats. 'Okay if I poke yer fire, Pat?' she said to the spluttering big lump. He didn't reply. Couldn't. His fire was grey like the rest of him. A glimmer in the ashes, though, that would come away and burn.

She roused the fire and added wood she collected at the riverside, kicking off the rats. 'Okay if I take a len o yer pot?' She took it over to the standpipe, rinsed it, held it under the tap again. The hard stream began to fill the pot and its changing music was like water she remembered long ago.

She borrowed his frying-pan as well. See men? When Rose died and one of his sisters took the boys and he finally walked out and left his house to fall down, he took a pot and a pan, a mug, a knife, fork and spoon and a blanket, all stuffed into a cobwebby khaki kitbag stencilled with a faded number and a name that wasn't Brady. 'See if I'd tried that?' she said. 'Cameron woulda called the cops. It's my crazy wife, officer, she's gone off with a nearly new frying-pan.' As it was, she didn't know to this day if he'd noticed she'd gone. A quick trawl round the top shelf of the newsagent's and that was him set up for the night. 'Could you fancy a sausage, Patrick?' she enquired. Brady woke up at that. Never known to fail.

'It's no that we hunt in packs,' she explained to the director, but somehow they all ended up near the Central Station, where it was warm or anyway dry. Lizzie went off to try her luck. It wouldn't be lucky for the guy, but you could tell that by looking at her, not much danger bodily fluids would be exchanged. Tam Ratface went off somewhere or other. He hadn't had any luck since the day he was born, in fact since his ma shagged a guy called Rattray whose name was a gift to the smartarses up and down the street. Belle and Brady found themselves in an alley, not exactly together, not exactly apart.

Slime underfoot and damp stone walls. The alley opened into a square littered courtyard. Empty barred windows and green corpse-light from the tall lamps on the bridge a mile overhead.

'Maybe this is it,' now-Belle said, looking on.

Brady went up and kicked a door but it stayed shut. 'Wis it no about here the old village wis meant tae be?' he said.

Maybe he said that. Maybe it was a voice in Belle's mind. 'You'll no believe this, Pat,' she said long ago. 'There's a guy comes into the library and he's gonny show me round the old village when his pal can get the key.'

'Oh aye. Take yer hatpin,' said Patrick with his arm round Rose. An engaged guy. Going to be married, if none too soon. He'd been known to peck a quick kiss on Rose's cheek in the street, never mind who might see.

'He's no that kind of guy. Cameron's his name,' she said.

Belle went off to find a dark corner and have a piss, and she should have told Pat to stay with the bags, because he had the same idea and went off another way. Naturally some kids came by and they were into the bags in seconds, rooting through them, grabbing them up to run away. She yelled, and she heard Brady shout to Kuwait, and fuck me but it was the dog that saved the day. He didn't like many people, and from his early life before Brady got him he sure as buggery didn't like kids. He came hurtling back and into them. There was yelping and howling and panting, and that was just the kids. The snapping and snarling came from Kuwait, hot on their heels.

'Thanks, pal,' said Belle as he galloped by.

Pat came strolling back and said 'Bastards'll no stop till they get tae Govan.' He'd been interrupted in his piss and hadn't got himself entirely sorted, but Belle hadn't the heart to mention it. He noticed it himself in a while.

'I could murder a Big Mac,' he remarked. Couldny haud the drink, okay, but bounced back like a yoyo every fuckin time, ready to eat his weight in chips. Strolling into the kitchen that very same fuck-you way, leaving the bedroom door wide open so that you could see as well as smell the reeking sheets. 'Nae food in the house, I don't suppose, naw?' Rose cast a shamed glance at Belle and scuttled to put on the chip-pan, and as she ran around she managed to shut the bedroom door.

'Whit did yer last servant die of?' Belle enquired.

'Aw, c'mon, Belle, hen.' Charming as fuck. Look at yerself, Patrick, said now-Belle, but it was a bit late in the day. He dug into a greasy pocket and found some coins. He'd been in the shopping mall again. It was guilt that did it, as they hurried to their cars with their load of plastic bags and nearly fell over this stinking old pile of shit with the dark eyes.

'Three-course dinner, sir? Bottla bubbly on the side?' She took the money and went off to the station kiosk. Of course there was only enough for one burger. When she had it in her hand, the sizzling brown meat and the tomato sauce and most of all the onions, it was too much for her and she ate it herself. Every scrap, and carefully wiped the grease from her mouth and hands.

Have tae tell him I lost the money. Nah, he'll never believe that. Okay, two kids nicked it. Two lassies. Whit's the world comin tae, Patrick, eh?

She sat on a bench and the destination board flickered over her head. It held the travelling crowds, it moved them. They'd rush on to the concourse with their tickets in their hands and stand there hopping with impatience, eyes raised to the board. Then flicker, flicker it would go, that's if it was working, and a whole chunk of the crowd would be sucked away like water down a stank. Platform thirteen for the Ayr line, platform five for East Kilbride, platform one for London. They never looked at Belle, which suited her fine.

She wasn't frightened what Pat would say about the burger. 'He's a gentle giant,' Rose whispered hopefully, and sure enough he'd never lifted a hand to her. (Never found out. And anyway she was ill by then.) Never would have went in for that kinky stuff that Cameron, getting desperate, tried. ('A husband and wife can do anything they like', he said, while Belle, arranging herself in the latest position he'd read about, said 'Depends on the husband. Depends on the wife.' No, she didn't say it of course, considering what he had in his hand.)

But it was jagging at her, what she'd done. Ate his fuckin burger! She sat there and felt it heavy and squirming inside her, making her fart. A woman in a sheepskin coat moved hastily to the next bench. A businessman perched on the extreme corner of Belle's bench since there was nowhere else to sit. 'Too late to say sorry now,' her father said, and she knew there was no hope. Rose, taking instruction to marry Pat, was quite pleased when she found out about confession. 'You can confess and then it's all right,' she reported, and she was thinking of their father, though he'd never been as hard on her as he was on Belle. She said it again years later, sitting with Danny on her knee. 'You can confess and it's all right.' Doubtfully now.

'Hey Belle,' Tam Ratface said in her ear, 'they'll no change this, dae you think, naw?'

'Now you've slabbered aw over it? Nae fuckin chance.'

'Canny stand ketchup. Forget tae tell them. Here.' Tam Ratface held the burger out to her and it actually wasn't too bad, just one toothmarked corner which could be cut away. A replacement burger. A miracle. 'This isny like you, Ratface,' she said. 'Are you no weel or whit?'

'Aw, very fuckin comical.' His breath stank like a pub toilet, which explained his lord of the manor attitude, though she couldn't make out how he'd managed to buy burgers and beer in the first place. 'Naw, naw, keep it, I'll place anither order.' He pulled a fistful of cash out of his torn pocket. 'Found a quid on the concourse,' he hurried to say, turning his back.

'Twenty quid that would be, but who's countin,' as she saw a fiver, and surely the brown corner of a tenner as well, caught up in the handful of change. More paper money rustled richly as he shoved the coins back into his pocket. 'Dumped the wallet, did you?' she said.

'Nearly aw credit cards,' he complained. 'Nae fuckin use. Nae possibility o tracin the owner, Belle. Platform one, the English train. Jumped oota some guy's back pocket. Hauf roads tae Liverpool afore I ever found the bastard.' He went cheerfully off towards the kiosk. 'Extra king-size, hold the ketchup,' she heard him say.

The miracle burger wasn't at all bad. She trimmed off the nibbled corner and took it back to Brady. 'Sorry I took a wee bite, couldny help masel,' she explained when he raised an eyebrow at the odd shape of the bun.

'Aw Christ, Belle, here, hae a bit.'

'Naw, ta, I'm on a diet.' He didn't know whether to take her seriously or not, but then he never did.

And that might have been okay, only he'd got hold of another fuckin bottle somewhere and it knocked him arse over tip. Wet nose, wet eyes, and out came the manky cardboard wallet with the photos. One more thing he'd stuffed in the kitbag when he hit the road. 'That's her wi the weans. That's her an me wi Kieron. That's us newly engaged. We'll get wan taken, Pat, she said, it'll mind us how it wis.'

'You were a fine-lookin couple, Patrick,' Belle said.

The wallet was brown and dry, cracking along the folds. The dim photographs, as Brady's brainless fingers tried to separate them, curled and clung. 'That's us at the coast when we were engaged. Single rooms, cost a fuckin bomb, but she wouldny take a double, what would they say, she said. Like she wasny three months along. They couldny tell to look at her right enough. Fuckin ridiculous, had tae nip along the corridor an back every fuckin night.'

'I'm just as glad she took the chance,' said Belle. And she very nearly meant it. 'Didny get much o it later on.'

Brady shifted fiercely on the cold stone. 'She didny mind. "Is that you away again?" was aw she'd say.'

Rose stood at the door, heavy with Kieron. No, it would be Danny. 'Ach, you've missed Pat again. Went aff at the weekend. Didny say when he'll be back.'

'Never does, does he?' No, she probably didn't say it, with Rose like that.

'Least he takes the dug wi him. Smelly brute an it'll no dae a thing for me.' That would be Derry or maybe Kabul.

'Some wives like the peace an quiet,' said Belle. 'So I've heard.'

'An she'd the weans,' Patrick eagerly explained. 'They're company, she'd say, on you go, they're nae trouble. She'd worry aboot Danny right enough. Fuckin stupid that wis. Strong as a fuckin carthorse frae day one.'

'She'd a hard time wi him an she wisny well,' said Belle sharply. 'A ten-pounder an a skelf like her.'

'Naw, hang on, a ten-pounder, Danny?' Brady wrinkled his nose. 'Sure he wis a seven-month wean.'

'Christ, you're no as daft as you look, Patrick,' Belle said. But daft enough not to notice her hesitating for a second there. 'Kieron wis the ten-pounder. Danny wis a preemie. I mind now.'

Brady sighed. 'That's as much as I dae mind. Oota ma skull the last six weeks.' He hunched his head between his shoulders. 'Couldny get near her. Know whit I mean.' She could hardly hear him. 'Okay when I'd a skinful. That's why I'd take it then.'

'Trouble wis when you'd only hauf a skinful.' His dark eyes came up, those daft long lashes and black eyebrows that hadn't gone grey. She'd said too much. That time, didny remember, never thought he would. 'That's whit you telt me anyway,' she said. 'That lassie in Manchester. That wis afore Danny. So you said.'

He swallowed. 'Went back there when Danny wis up a bit. Would you credit it, that bitch slammed the door in ma face?'

'So Rose got you back again,' said Belle without expression. 'Couldny believe her luck, I daresay.'

She'd pushed him too hard. He snuffled and snivelled, awash with grief. 'Shouldny have went away an left her, Belle. Didny know when I wis well aff. The wee problem but. Couldny seem to kick it. Bombed every fuckin night.'

'You're sometimes no as bad as this.'

'I come an go,' he said. 'The way Rose went, that hit me hard.' She heard the shake in his voice. 'Any fuckin swally that hadny the skull an crossbones. Whiles I wouldny care if it had.'

He stared at her. Dark eyes in a bristly old wino's face. All at once he snatched up the cardboard wallet and spilled photographs on to his knee. 'That's her wi Danny. That's Kieron an Danny when they were at school.' The last one, well crumpled, stuck in its cardboard slot. Young Rose in her white lacy dress, cunningly swagged across the front so you could hardly tell. Though everybody knew. Patrick impossible in suit and tie.

'Your fuckin hair, boy,' said Belle. It was smarmed down and there was a parting, never seen before or since.

'Didny last the night,' Brady recalled.

'Well, it wouldny, would it.' It would fall over his brow as he danced with the bridesmaid, which he had to do. 'Fine-lookin couple,' she said, and knew she'd said it before.

'Ah Jesus, Belle, she wis a flower.' His black and white hair fell over his eyes the same way.

And suddenly he was asleep, knocked out by the gin and the tears. Belle sitting with the photographs in her hand. Sorry, Pat, the dug ate them. But he'd slit the bastard open to get them back. Kuwait watched her closely as she tucked them back in their wallet and slid the wallet into Brady's inside pocket above his fluttering heart.

'Teatime,' she said to Kuwait. 'Ratface canny possibly have got through that wad yet.' But in the station with its cold light and clanging, quacking noises she found Ratface slumped in a red plastic bucket seat and knew she'd come too late.

'Gonny get us a portion o chips, Belle?'

She stood and looked down at him. 'Fuck that for a game,' she said. 'Where's it went?'

'Somebody nicked it. I gied it back tae the guy. It's feenished,' he whined. Chip-grease and soy sauce dabbled his jacket and he'd puked up over his knees. She saw the leavings of the beer in his bloody eyes and broken-out face. 'Aw but a fiver. I'm keepin that.'

'So get yer ain fuckin chips,' she said, turning away.

'I'm keeping it fur a wumman,' he whispered in the echoing great concourse under the station roof.

She turned back and looked at him crouched in the perforated red chair. Design award winner, specially for stations, so the next happy traveller wouldn't sit down in a puddle of Tam Rattray's piss. He shifted under her stare and had a try, that nearly worked, at straightening his spine.

'Canny find one I fancy,' he said.

She saw him very clearly on his lonely walk through the town, up Bath Street with the cars cruising slowly in the night, round Blythswood Square where the short-skirted lassies were. The worst hackit dogface among them would turn away.

Just as clearly she saw Pat Brady flat out, rat-arsed, asleep, with his magpie hair and white face. Though the house was down years ago, she saw the closemouth where Kieron and Danny were arguing the toss, that time she dropped round to see Rose and found Pat was back from his travels for maybe a day or two.

'Auntie Belle, Auntie Belle,' yelled Danny who was four, 'he came back hauf an hoor ago an he said we're no tae move from here an I'm needin to pee, can I no go up there?'

'Jesus, boy, are you tired o livin?' said Kieron, and you wouldn't mistake whose son he was. 'He'll bung you a quid when he comes oot. Dae it in the syver,' so Danny hauled out his wee thing and piddled in the gutter, and off they went down the street, never looking back. She climbed the three flights, drawn upwards stair by stair.

They hadn't shut the storm door. Why would they, a man and wife? The inside door was warped away from its frame and she could hear. She heard Rose laughing. She went back downstairs so silently they never knew.

'A fiver?' she said to Tam Ratface. 'Come on an we'll talk aboot it, okay?' She led him out of the station. Wrang guy but it's no as if it's the fuckin first time, now-Belle said.

But they were up on the green grass again, under the trees. Nowhere near the station. 'This canny be right,' Belle said, 'how did I get here?'

'Well, that's what we all want to know, love,' the director said.

There were two doors in the square. The broken one wouldn't open if she tried and anyway she wasn't going there. But the high nail-studded west door wasn't right either. A shadow swung over and she turned, but on the tall lamp-standard hung only the bird and the tree and the fish and the bell.

'What's the matter with Belle?'

'She doesn't know,' drawled the voice-over man.

'Doesn't need to know.'

'I'm fuckin lookin for it,' she said, but Pat Brady said 'You'll no find it here.'

The cameraman crooked an arm and consulted his watch, which he wore poncily on the inside of his wrist. 'Not sure how long we've got, love, before the light goes.' The doors batted briefly in a little cold breeze.

'Tell you what,' coaxed the director, 'why not do this instead?'

'It's no right. It's no what I'm lookin for,' she said, but they closed in behind her and crowded her through the cathedral door.

3

From the air, up under the roof-beams, she looked right along the nave, a road between eight-sided trees. They'd got to the editing stage. The programme was running on a screen high up in the clerestory. Didn't seem to be saying anything new. They were thinking of calling it *A Lost Lady* now.

'Hellova fantoosh,' she said. The director sighed and raised a hand and a researcher came running up with a phrasebook. 'Fantoosh,' she read. 'Pretentious or showy. We're going to need subtitles.' And for a while they ran the programme with subtitles, till Belle found out how to do it and subtitled Cameron's speeches, wah-wah-wah, and Cameron went absolutely spare.

John Knox was up at the front, in the pulpit, spouting away, dinging the pulpit in blads. She saw his fist thump down, the dry old wood crack, the splinters fly. And yet it was not consumed, so Belle went up and took an axe to it. Brady straddled in front of it and pissed on the burning bush. Didn't make a blind bit of difference as far as she could see. Behind John Knox was the priest who used to visit Patrick Brady's primary school and quiz them on the catechism. 'I'm telling my uncle you got belted,' said Pat's smug cousin Margaret, Belle's pal. 'You never answered one question. You never even tried.'

'Fuckin arse-bandit,' said Brady, ten years old, and slung his rosary beads at Father Columba. They spun through the air like a gaucho's bolas and garrotted Father, who fell on top of John Knox and brought the pulpit crashing down.

'Sit down and listen,' somebody said.

'The fuck I will.' But she was swooping down to sit beside Cameron in the front pew. 'Naw, come on,' she said, 'this isny who I am.'

'Oh, sorry, Belle, we thought it was.'

They were up on the hill of the Necropolis, the city of the dead. John Knox on his pillar, as high as a tenement block, a thousand times more important than Belle. More respectable than Cameron, even. 'Fond o shaggin under-age lassies,' Belle observed. 'Marrying them in fact. "Are you ready?" he'd say.'

The cliff-face of the cathedral below them, spires and tenements beyond, all black in the smoky fog. And the tall factory stalks breathing fire, and the panting steam engines, and half a million little chimney-pots smoking in the town. An iron grate and bone-cold quick fingers working to build a fire. Crumpled-up paper, a wigwam of kindling, small coal. The flare of the match and its hot familiar smell. An iron ball came swinging across and knocked it all down. Light behind the fog.

They walked down the path, which was the hard grey cathedral nave. 'Maybe it's there,' the director said.

'No, no, no, no. Those days are gone and a good thing too.' That was Cameron, raised up and certain in the pulpit, in the black gown of John Knox, preaching how things should be.

'How they've aye been,' said Belle.

'How they've always been,' he corrected her, smirking. 'I'm sure they didn't teach you *aye* at the Academy.'

'Taught us fuck all in that dump.'

'I really don't know where you picked up that language,' Cameron said. Though sometimes in the dark he asked for it and sometimes it worked.

'You know fine, ya stupid cunt,' said Belle.

The minister thumped the pulpit. The teacher banged his hard black tawse on the desk, and there was Cameron smiling patiently in John Knox's Geneva gown. 'How things have always been,' he said. 'How we want them always to be.'

'No me,' said Belle. Behind her the breaker's ball swung over the roofs.

The director leaned out of the TV set in the clerestory and said 'Is this what you're looking for, Belle?'

'Is it fuck.'

'Oh, it's all right, she's found what she was looking for,' said Cameron, settling down with his pipe. 'This is how things are. How they've always been.' The city crashed around his head but he waved his pipe and it stood up again. Red and black tenements in the fog. 'Always have been and always will be. Our children will rise up and call us blessed.'

'Whit fuckin children?' said Belle.

The programme was running on a loop. There went Cameron smoking his pipe and Queen Victoria riding by. There shambled Brady, jamming a greasy bunnet over wisps of piebald hair. There was Belle shagging him, and dancing on a plinth, and bare scuddy under the cold dawn sky. 'What we want to know is how you got here, Belle,' they said.

'That's easy,' she said, 'just walked oot one day.'

'No. Before that. What are you looking for?'

'Cobbles, pavements, houses, shops,' said Cameron, 'all still there.'

'It's your fault,' said the doctor in the pulpit. No, it was John Knox. Was it Cameron's dad? 'Your fault. What you did, or what you failed to do.'

'*Mea culpa, mea culpa, mea maxima culpa*,' Belle said, and John Knox went ballistic, wrong language, wrong faith. The high west door swung open and there stood Patrick Brady, twenty-three years old and what a smasher, with his black hair and dark eyes. 'Never seem tae see you thae days, Belle,' he said.

'I work two evenings a week,' she said, 'and there's the night school, and I've got to hoover the place some time.'

He sniffed like a drain, because now he was this old guy shambling across the wasteground. He turned to aim a cuff at the dog Kuwait, which was never going to connect, never intended to. 'You canny come in here, ya stupid cunt,' he said. Kuwait panted, adoring him.

'No dogs, no children, no Irish need apply,' said Cameron. 'Don't you know this is a church? A library? A respectable house?'

'Like fuck it is,' said Belle, and Pat turned and clicked his fingers and all the dogs of his life came bouncing in, Kuwait and Kabul and Derry and Saigon and Yang. The thing about Brady's dogs was they were always the same, lean black collie crosses that loved Brady and hated everybody else. They gambolled up the nave, and he came with them, and it was hard to see whether he was a smelly old wanker, or a kid with his hand stuck out to get the belt and his bottom lip caught on his teeth, or a young guy with black eyes like the light in the coals. The eyes, actually, stayed the same.

Up in the nave they were starting to sing a psalm, but Belle, looking for something, found a low dim stair. It led down into the crypt. It turned under broad arches and a faint light glimmered on the edge of each step. She came out into a forest of pillars. The oldest stone in the whole cathedral stood quietly by the wall. Still not far enough down.

But too far below. On top of these pillars stood the cathedral floor. On that floor, the great tree pillars of the nave. On those pillars, the roof and the steeple, and all of it pressing down on Belle. She felt it, the heavy great building, the old city, weighted on her head. She choked, she began to cry.

The reasearcher rushed up with a guidebook and the director remarked chattily, as if she'd known it all along, 'Owing to the steep gradient of the site, one end of the crypt is above ground. There are windows, see?'

'Silly girl,' said Cameron.

'Silly cunt,' said Belle, and breathed the fresh air at the east end. Darkness, bad air, somebody crying. Is that what I'm looking for? St Mungo's well blinked a dark wet eye, like Patrick's on a bad day. She dropped a stone in but no splash ever came.

There was a door at the east end of the crypt. No, a park gate, curlicued and green. Trees sprang up as Belle walked towards it, and a row of red sandstone terrace houses that stepped up the hill with stained-glass flowers in their doors.

Here in the park the TV crew were right at home. Squirrels and Shakespeare on the grass and heavy summer trees. They strutted in their flares and mullets and Zapata moustaches, sometimes distressed jeans, sometimes cargo pants, and they swigged their cappuccinos and skinny lattes, leaving them half-finished by the side of the path. The shilpit wee ned Tam Ratface nicked them and drank them before they were completely cold. He didn't think much of the house-trained guys who emptied the dregs into the grass and tossed the cardboard cups into a bin.

'We'll have to edit this down,' the director said. 'Twenty years is too long.'

'That's the whole fuckin point,' said Belle.

She went up the path to the flagpole and the general sat high on his curvetting horse, though that was in a different park. The early streetlights pricking out from the river to the braes, all over the endless city view. Rose stood beside her, a ghost.

'She should have died hereafter,' said the actor down on the lawn, and Belle said 'You shoulda died a lot sooner, ya stupid cunt.' John Knox and Father Columba both made for her on that and she dodged them with ease, but in front of her stood a wee girl in a fairisle jumper and school skirt, holding her toddling sister by the hand. She couldn't dodge them. 'I didny say that, Rose,' she said. 'That wisny me.'

'Oh, sorry, Belle, we thought it was.'

Along the path came Pat Brady and his dog. No, two of his dogs, because dogs don't live for twenty years. These two hadn't both been around at the same time and so they kept melting and morphing into one dog, but they were probably Derry and Kabul. They frisked ahead of him and squatted on the smooth-mown grass. A parkie, a west-end wife,

Cameron, John Knox rushed in from all directions and drove them away. 'Can the fuckin dug no take a shit tae itsel?' said Brady, and you could kind of see his point.

'We still want to know how you got here, Belle.'

'Where?'

'Good question,' the director allowed. 'Here.' She nodded across the park at the red terraces.

'Thought you said this bit's too long awready.'

'We'll do a montage. How you got here and –' She nodded at Brady. 'How you got there. And why.'

'You canny ask me that,' Belle said.

'Oh yes, we can ask, Belle. Can you answer, though?'

They'd got another working title for the programme, *West End to Wasteground*. It was running on a TV set slung on a wire above the river that plunged and tumbled through the park. The voice-over man butted in ('It's all coming together,' the director said in satisfaction, and Belle said 'I wish'), booming out portentous lines that really didn't fit, as even the director could hear. 'Perhaps Belle thought she could rescue him from the streets? Or perhaps a happy ending in cardboard city was what she had in mind?'

'Lie back an mind the dogshit,' said Belle. Down on the lawn the actor said 'Love is not love which alters when it alteration finds,' and that wasn't even in a play.   Pat said to Kabul, because he had nobody else to talk to, 'Cervical cancer. The doctor telt me how that happens. My fuckin fault.'

'Or Danny's dad's fault,' said Belle. But no, she couldn't say that. 'Or nae cunt's fault. It's no always because o that.'

'The doctor telt me.'

'Fuckin doctors,' said Belle. She threw half a brick at the red terrace house where the doctor lived, but the stained glass was elastic as toffee and bounced it right back. It missed Pat but he fell down anyway. Flat on his face, crying, in the dogshit and the mud. 'Look after him for God's sake,' Belle said to Kabul, and Kabul licked Patrick's stubbly jaw.

Cameron was upright and solemn in his black suit, white shirt, black tie, and she was in her blacks as well. Somebody, probably one of the five sisters, had straightened Pat out and hosed him down and got him into a suit and stood him in the reception line. You could still smell the drink off him through the mothballs and the extra strong mints. Cameron shook his hand with fastidious fingertips and waited for Belle to do the same.

Instead she hugged Patrick, couldn't help it, and he hugged her, fierce and helpless, crying down her neck.

Everybody was very welcome somewhere or other for tea and ham rolls, but Cameron simply couldn't spare the time to take her and anyway she didn't think Pat would be there. 'It finished you, boy,' she said. 'Your fault or no. The thought it mighta been.'

'We still don't know why you're here,' the director said. 'You'll have to help us, Belle.'

'I'll dae my best,' she said. 'I can dae nae fuckin mair.'

'Is that the best you can do?' said Cameron, and leathered her bum, which fortunately seemed to work for once and she got some peace after that. They came out through the curlicued green park gate and crossed the road. Ten steps up to the door with the stained-glass flowers, that wasn't right, never had been.

4

Now-Belle was observing then-Belle, and the trouble was that then-Belle couldn't be pinned down, shape-shifting over the long, long twenty years from a slim tall girl with a mop of red hair to something bony and crisply coiffed. 'Montage, it's the only way,' the director wailed, and up came Cameron in his little tartan drawers, and Belle behind the library counter, and Cameron handcuffing Belle to the bedposts, and Patrick drunk as a skunk. 'We couldn't do it without you, Belle,' the director assured her.

'As long as you're no sayin this is me.'

'Oh sorry, we thought it was.'

Summer in the west end, heavy green trees. Ten steps up to a white-painted door, tall purple tulips flowering in the glass. 'Whit happened? It wis aw gonny change,' protested Belle. 'Knocked the whole fuckin place doon so they did. Knock it doon, age of Aquarius, make it new. Tights an miniskirts. Cappuccino. Permissive society. We did aw that. Whit happened here?'

'Why, nothing happened here,' Cameron said with pride.

'Fuckin right. No since eighteen ninety-five.'

'Ninety-seven,' corrected Cameron, title deeds in hand.

'All right, let's move along now,' the director said. 'Your wedding, Belle. Church wedding, was it?'

'According to the ordinances of the established presbyterian church of Scotland,' said Belle, 'and Cameron bein Cameron, we got tae hire the cathedral. Wouldny really be legally valid otherwise, Cameron's mum let us understand.'

'That's good. We've got footage of the exterior.'

'Never been as cauld in ma fuckin life,' said Belle. 'An rush-bottomed chairs. Fortunately the bride disny sit down much. Patrick said he had the pattern on his arse for a week.'

She was standing in front of John Knox in her satin and tulle, with Cameron in his kilt and velvet jacket and lacy jabot. 'You were a lovely girl, Belle,' said the director in unfeigned surprise.

'Aye, well, the red hair.'

'Taller than Cameron too.'

'Plus I had the balls.'

Hardly anybody on the bride's side of the church. 'My mother's dead,' she explained to Cameron's frosty mum. 'My father's somewhere around.' Likely pestering the bridesmaid, who was Belle's pal from work. Rose thought she'd look funny in the photographs ten months pregnant, and besides she was a Catholic now.

Pat and Rose were in the congregation and Rose kept Patrick right, made sure he didn't kneel down or anything, which wouldn't have played well with Cameron's mum. Or with Cameron, come to that. 'The cathedral's really yours,' Belle had said, laughing, at a pre-wedding get-together, and Patrick quite liked the idea. Cameron didn't. Told Belle off in the car afterwards. 'What was that you were saying? The cathedral used to be a Catholic church? Where on earth did you get an idea like that?'

Rose was pretty obvious of course (they hid her in the back row of the family group) and many were the jokes directed at Cameron and Belle. Now you're married we wish you joy, first a girl and then a boy! May all your troubles be little ones! Belle's old aunt, who'd insisted on coming though everybody thought she was dead, recited at the reception 'Never mind whit Cammy says, keep yer goonie ower yer taes,' but fortunately nobody on Cameron's side understood a single word.

Cameron was anxious to get her nightgown up. Well, he'd nobly held off right through their engagement, that's to say after the episode which had started it all. Which wasn't to be talked about, Belle quite understood that. When she came out of the en suite bathroom in their honeymoon hotel Cameron was revealed in little tartan pants, a different tartan from his kilt. 'Mum's fault,' he said when he saw Belle looking at them. 'She hadn't time to take them back. Nobody's going to see them but you. Oh, I'll get a refund, don't you worry,' he added.

'It's not that,' she said, staring still.

'Well, I didn't want to give you too much of a shock, dear.' Off they came and it was a bit of a shock. Sixty-watt bulbs in Belle's bedsit, and during the episode which they didn't mention she'd been too excited to notice much. But they were married now, so high-wattage lights, keep them all on. Anything they felt like doing was all right, though not to be talked about, of course. 'Are you ready?' Cameron enquired.

'I don't know.' But he was, which was all that mattered, it seemed.

'Skip a bit here,' the director. 'Happy marriages are boring.'

'Fuck me, that explains it,' said Belle.

She walked along the brick-laid path in the narrow back garden behind the house with the stained-glass door, which stretched into a mother-of-pearl mist. 'There must be more than this,' she said.

'I don't want any more than this,' said Cameron.

'Well, I do.'

The director was getting twitchy. Nothing happening at all. 'Canny help it,' said Belle. 'Wanted something. Didny know whit.' And none of her troubles were little ones. 'You'll have no time to be bored then,' Cameron's mum made sure to let her know.

'Meanwhile,' said Belle, 'I had ma work. "Does Cameron not mind?" people asked a lot.' A wee job in the library, Tuesday and Thursday mornings, date-stamping Mills and Boons. She'd passed her exams and they wanted her full time, but the trouble was that in a permanent post she'd have to work shifts, and so she wouldn't always have been home to make Cameron's tea.

The camera panned round to the door of the reading room, though it didn't venture in. 'Smellyvision,' said the cameraman. 'I'd rather go to Afghanistan.' The old men and women shuffled out to ask for magazines, which had to be asked for since they'd just be vandalised if they were out on the shelves. An old woman thin as a thread with clean grey hair tucked under a felt beret. An old man with his feet at right angles to his shinbones and blue, blue eyes. Belle saw him out in the street one afternoon and said hello. Cameron was appalled.

'But I know him,' she said, 'he comes in every day.'

'You don't have to *speak* to him.'

'Yes I do.' It was now-Belle who saw a black-haired guy, not so old but no longer very young, lurching across the square.

'So it would be a Wednesday or Friday,' said the director, gamely keeping up, 'when you visited Rose. Or a Monday, I suppose.'

'Nae chance. Washin day.'

'Or a weekend. Then Cameron could have gone with you.'

'You really haveny got the fuckin picture, have yez?' said Belle.

So Wednesday or Friday, didn't matter, the door was always open, that was Pat and Rose. 'Thought you wouldn't mind me dropping in,' she'd say, though they were three stairs up and dropping in would involve the SAS.

'A real old tenement flat!' said the director, all excited, and up it sprang, coal fire and kitchen bed and pulleys hung with damp clothes. Bright enough, a bit cluttered, family photos and a faintly smelly bed for the current dog, Derry it would be at that time. Not to mention all the Sacred Hearts and Infants of Prague donated by Patrick's sisters. A saintly Pope looked down on Rose sitting by the fire singing to Kieron on her knee. 'Ah, you've missed Pat again,' she'd say.

'Never mind. Saw this in the sales, thought it might do Kieron.'

'It's lovely! Look at that, Kieron! Your daddy'll be over the moon!'

When he comes back. If he's sober. Rose never said any of that, and neither did Belle of course. He'd always been a bit that way inclined and you could hardly expect him to stop all of a sudden, even his sisters agreed. Still went down the pub with his pals, always had. Going away for a week, two weeks at a time, that was something new, however. That accounted for Rose's pale face and the lines between her brows.

'I wouldny have him different,' she said. Must have been another time, later on. 'Sure I miss him when he's away, but aw, Belle, when he comes back, you canny imagine.'

The trouble was that Belle could imagine very well.

'Let's not go into that,' the director said.

'Ah, c'mon.'

'I'm just keeping an eye on the storyline. The next thing was the baby question, yah?'

'You'll want me wi ma feet up in stirrups and ma privates on parade?'

'I don't think –' the director whimpered, but there Belle was, and John Knox was a doctor now in a white coat.

'What seems to be the trouble, Mrs Cameron?'

'Mrs Campbell,' said Belle for the umpteenth time. She was Mrs Cameron Campbell and people were always getting it wrong. Mrs Cameron, though, she thought, that's right enough. I'm Mrs Cameron. That's who I am. Not Belle.

'I can't get pregnant.'

'You're encountering some problems in achieving conception. Well, we'd better find out why, hadn't we?'

'What are you looking for, Belle?' said the TV screen above, reflecting the bright instruments, the gloved hands.

'Relax. Are you ready?'

'I don't know.'

'I don't see any reason for it,' he said, 'so it must be your fault.'

'It's perfectly possible it's down to the man,' said the gentle Irish nurse, but Cameron snapped 'Not in this case,' and the doctor said 'Not in this case. It's your fault, Belle.'

They wrapped that scene and the cameraman, looking a bit green, went out for a smoke. 'Now up tae Rose's again,' Belle said. The director looked doubtful, because they'd just been there, but when Belle explained, she said 'Dramatic irony!' and called the cameraman back.

'Things has changed,' said Belle, 'Pat's home for once in a way,' and she climbed the stairs, passing Rose's friendly downstairs neighbour, the red-haired guy who was handier than Pat with a screwdriver and never grudged the time. He favoured Belle with a nervous smile.

Patrick and the dog (probably Kabul by now) were in charge, looking after Kieron, because Rose was at the doctor's. 'Oh right, she told me, I forgot,' Belle said, but Patrick didn't hear her. He was so excited. Sober as a judge but eyes like dark stars. 'She thinks she's expectin again,' he said.

'Does she,' said Belle. The calendar on the wall yelled at her but she wouldn't look at it, didn't dare. She wouldn't say 'Just back from your travels, aren't you, Pat? How long's that you've been away?'

And Patrick, well, you always knew he was as thick as mince. 'Just got back on Saturday an we, y'know, right away' (extremely mealy-mouthed Pat was in those days, anyway when sober and in front of Belle) 'an bingo!' He was so pleased. 'Never knew you could tell that soon. But she rung up the doctor, got an appointment, he'll dae a test, she says.'

He didn't know where to put himself for excitement. He marched about the wee kitchen, swinging Kieron to the ceiling and swinging him down, in a high old state, going to be a daddy again. 'Long trip that yin, got the length o Manchester this time, but that's it, I'm back to stay. Plenty o jobs around. Get oota this dump.'

'There's houses going in Wolfhill.' Where there's no pubs. She didn't say that.

'Fuck Wolfhill. They murder kittens up there. Sure they do, son?' he said to Kieron, who adored him like Kabul.

'The nice bit of Wolfhill.'

'There's nae nice bits in Wolfhill. Naw, Cumbernauld, East Kilbride, great hooses there, three bedrooms, gardens, we'll get a car an come an visit yez, Belle.'

An no a drop will pass your lips, Patrick, frae this day on. Belle could have said that. And she could have said that Rose couldn't, the doctor couldn't, nobody could, reliably tell she was pregnant that soon after the act. That anyway she'd made the doctor's appointment two weeks ago. Look at the fuckin calendar, Patrick Brady, she could have said. Count how long you've been away. Ask Rose straight. She'll no be able tae tell you a flat-out lie.

'This could drag a bit,' the director complained.

'Dae it wi graphics,' said Belle. 'That's whit Patrick needed. A blackboard an pointer. A pocket calculator.' But she skipped what she did say to Pat. The congratulations, the teasing, when Rose came home. And how he looked standing there in the kitchen laughing with delight. Cut to where she climbed the steps again to her own stained-glass door.

'This'll no drag,' she promised. 'After the watershed stuff this'll be.' Because somewhere about now she stopped even pretending she was interested in going to bed with Cameron. 'An that didny have a very good effect on Cameron,' she said. 'He stopped bein able to dae it at aw.'

'Hmm,' the director said, though the cameraman got her drift and reloaded his camera in a great hurry, in case he missed something good.

'If I was you,' Belle said to them, 'I would hae an outside shot o the house. Red sandstone terrace. Quiet street. Summer, flowers, trees, the birds an the bees. Ironic, okay, that'll get you brownie points at the BAFTAs. Stained-glass front door. In the door an up the stairs. Close-up of the bedroom door. The door swings open –'

'Yes, Belle, I'm the director here.'

But the cameraman was right up there: 'And inside –'

'An inside,' said Belle, 'depends whit magazines he picked up on the way home. An which o his pals he saw at the Masons last night. The handcuffs an the tawse, nae problem. The dogcollar I'm no so sure, maybe he had tae go intae the pet shop himself. Christmas present for Rover, don't you know. The suspender belt, how he got that I do not know. Quite huffy when I telt him I didny hae one, been in tights since nineteen sixty-six.'

'You see, Belle,' the director said, rather worried, 'we're verging on domestic abuse here.'

'Is that a fact,' said Belle.

'Did it do the trick?' the cameraman wanted to know.

'No very often,' Belle said. 'Didny stop him tryin but.'

The director said 'All right, yah, I get the picture, this is actually going to work quite well. Heavy on the west end ambience. Respectable house. And inside –'

'Voice over,' suggested Belle. 'Cameron's voice, "Between husband and wife anything goes." God, wis I fuckin fed up hearin that. An inside, the two o us concentratin aw our god-given powers on six inches o gristle, willin it to gie a feeble twitch. You might get a wee laugh there.'

'Six inches?' said the cameraman, and the director made a note.

'I never fuckin measured,' said Belle irritably. 'It's a figure o speech.'

They got busy on that. Time passed, spring, summer, autumn, and during this time nothing did the trick for Cameron more than once or twice, not the handcuffs nor the suspender belt nor the tawse nor talking dirty in the dark. 'It's getting a bit heavy,' said the director, though the cameraman was having the time of his life.

'Right, let's lighten it up,' said Belle. 'Yez'll like this.' A ring and then a knocking at the stained-glass door, and she knew before she opened it who it was and what kind of state he was in. Kabul panted eagerly at his feet.

'You're steamboats, Pat.'

'Canny help it. Rose's due any day.'

'Would she not be glad of your company?' Maybe not, right enough, since he seemed to have pissed his pants. She took him in, gave him a blanket, threw his things in the washing-machine feeling quite like the mum on the telly, though that understanding lady usually had to deal with nice clean mud. None of Cameron's leisurewear came near being Patrick's size. 'Sit there and behave yourself,' she said, and gave him a cup of coffee which he immediately spilled into his lap. Thanks to the blanket no major injury was sustained, though naturally he had to check.

'You're in a terrible state, Patrick,' she said. 'It's really no fair on Rose.'

'I haveny been able tae get near her for six weeks,' he whined.

'Jesus God, Patrick, are you a man or –' No, scrub that. That was the whole problem of course. 'How did you manage last time?' she enquired.

'It was okay last time. She let me – We got to –'This time she's no weel an the doctor says –'

'Well, you could surely – You could – Would you like to have a word with Cameron?' God, she must be losing her mind. 'Could you not do it yourself? That's what Cameron does.' Yes, definitely lost touch with reality. And the trouble was that Pat took an interest in this imaginary scenario. She'd have thought he would sympathise with Cameron, but no, he sympathised with her, which she absolutely didn't need. And he was still so pissed he didn't know where to stop.

'Whit I canny understand, Belle, neither can Rose, is why you merriet the fucker in the first fuckin place. You didny hae to merry him.'

'I had to marry somebody,' said Belle. 'Thought I had to. And where were you?'

She couldn't possibly have said that. She had, because Patrick was preparing an answer with the solemn deliberation of the very drunk. 'I wis merriet tae Rose awready,' he gravely pointed out.

'Get back to her!' she screamed. 'She's needing you!' She jumped to her feet, and so did he, and the blanket fell off. He was ready, God, not half. Couldny haud it but it never put him off his food, or off the other thing. He grabbed her and slabbered a wet kiss on her mouth. 'Aw c'mon, Belle. I've always liked you,' he said.

She made it to the kitchen. Thumped the switches of the washer-drier. Hauled out his trousers and pants. 'They're no dry yet,' he objected, but she yelled 'Get them on!' He modestly turned his back and obeyed. Just as well, because wouldn't this be the day Cameron came home early from work? That would have to occur.

The cameraman couldn't film for laughing. 'You're making this up,' he said.

'I fuckin wish,' said Belle.

So there was Cameron with his latest top-shelf magazine tucked under his arm, and there was Patrick Brady with his trousers on, if only just, but still absolutely steamboats, stotious, miraculous, falling-over drunk. 'Cameron's fury knew no bounds,' said the voice-over man hopefully, though all Belle could actually remember him saying was 'This is a respectable house! Get out of here and don't come back!'

'Okay,' said Pat amiably. Belle stood at the window and watched him lolloping, staggering, tripping over Kabul, half-falling and recovering, all the way down the leafy west end street. She didn't suppose he'd remember much when he sobered up. Maybe not anything at all.

Cameron looked at his watch and led her upstairs. He'd been reading about something else which wasn't very respectable at all and left her with a sore arse, and she was glad to find that he still couldn't get it up.

The cameraman blew out his cheeks and took a break to change his film. The director said 'Yes, well. Now we'll draw back, out of the bedroom, down the stairs, out of the stained-glass door –'

'No yet. We're no finished yet. Then Rose died,' said Belle.

'Ah yes. We've had the funeral. We covered that.'

'Yez asked how I got here. Okay. Rose died. We had the funeral. Pat disappeared aff the radar. I went tae the shops wan day an I thought I seen him. Definite I did.'

And there came Brady, shambling across the wasteground as they'd seen him before. You could only recognise him because of Kabul. His hair was so greasy you could hardly tell the colour, but his stubbly chin had white bristles among the black. Totally knackered, totally done. It was then-Belle who stood watching him, but now-Belle had tears in her eyes as well.

'We're still asking what you thought you could do for him,' the director quite meekly said.

'Yez can ask that till yer nose bleeds,' Belle said. 'There isny an answer tae that.'

Back to the west end house. Cameron quite excited with a new project in hand. 'Role-playing,' explained Belle, and there they were, Belle in a frilly apron and fishnets and a suspender belt, still with lovely legs. Cameron in his father's pinstripes and stiff shirt. 'Now you're to say this,' he instructed her, and gave out a sentence in French. '"Oh, have mercy, master" is what it means.'

Belle said 'Vieux cochon,' which wasn't what he'd said. The director and the cameraman both looked blank but the voice-over man snickered like a donkey. 'It means dirty old man, only ruder,' he said.

'Learnt us something at the Academy efter aw,' Belle said. 'He got the jail eventually for interferin wi Three B.'

'So you role-played with Cameron,' the director gamely pursued.

'It didny dae anything for him. I felt a wee bit sorry for him that night,' Belle said. 'Funny that.'

Silence for a moment or two while the camera whirred. 'But no enough tae stay,' she said.

The director ventured at last, 'Er, Belle, we're still trying to find out why.'

'I'm lookin for something, ya stupid cunt,' said Belle.

There was a whole raft of doors in the corner of the bedroom where Cameron lay weeping on the bed. A broken door, but she wasn't going there. A very old door with a peephole two-thirds of the way up that a tall girl like Belle could look through.

'No, we've still got a bit to do before that,' the director said.

So there was a very fancy door in beaten brass with flowers and leaves and spooky women curling round its thick small glass panes, and there was a library door, easily recognised because it said SILENCE in big letters, painted gilt. And the old door with the peephole wouldn't go away. Those three doors shimmered together, sometimes three, sometimes one. Belle walked forward and went through them. Or through it, she probably ought to say.

5

And the TV crew were really getting above themselves. They'd found yet another title, *One Hand Clapping*. 'Eh?' said Belle. But it fitted the wild things, the changing things, the sixties things that were going on. They had trouble finding somewhere to rig up the TV set. Every time they got it hitched to a building a wrecker's ball came swinging through and knocked the whole place down.

They did a sweep of the Gorbals, from raggedy kids playing all across the wide carless streets that dwindled into the pearly mist, to those same kids, inquisitive, big-eyed, watching the houses fall. One of them was Lizzie with her raggedy drawers hanging down. Another was Tam Ratface. Quite cute then.

Out of the wrecked city grew poetry and art, and guitars crashed their chords around the coffee-bars. 'Did you swing, Belle?' the director said.

'I wis too fuckin busy haudin on.'

The cameraman overdosed on miniskirts. 'Like you've never seen legs before,' the director said, a trifle bemused. 'Like you never saw Kylie's bum.'

'Ah, but they hadn't. Not out in the street. I'm trying to show what they saw.' Camera angles all over the place. 'Those legs go all the way up!' crooned the cameraman.

'Did ya think they useta stop?' enquired Belle.

Skirts that skimmed the cheeks of your arse, the reason tights came in. The reason Belle didn't have a suspender-belt when Cameron required one. 'Concealing yet revealing,' intoned the voice-over man, and the cameraman nodded eagerly, seizing on a sociological point. Well, an excuse to poke his lens up lassies' skirts. 'So whit else is new?' said Belle.

'And the pill. And the abortion act,' the director said.

'Just as fuckin well wi aw thae legs on the warpath,' said Belle. 'Did I mention why Rose got merriet? Why I did, come tae that? You wouldny believe it now.'

That actually worried the director quite a bit. 'No, you wouldn't,' she said. 'You could have – I know you wanted, um, wanted a boyfriend, but –'

'There wis this night in ma bedsit,' said Belle.

'You didn't have to marry him for fuck's sake,' said the director.

'Well put,' said Belle.

But the director had lost her cool and coffee bars sprang up all over the place. And minis, and the air was sweet with wacky baccy, and the Beatles played their innocent sexy songs. And got banned for *Norwegian Wood*. 'It says here –' the researcher butted in.

'See, the trouble was we hadny read it, where I wis,' said Belle.

There she was, a redhead, a tall girl, with the legs all right and the rest of the equipment as well. On her way to work, in the library, on her way home, frying rissoles on a beat-up green gas cooker in her bedsit with a frown of concentration between her eyes. 'Two evenings shift work an the night school an I had to hoover the place an wash ma smalls. I hadny the time tae swing,' said Belle. And the frown, the Fair Isle cardigan, the book under her arm put them off anyway. 'Got a mini when I started seein Cameron,' she said. 'Fuckin impossible tae get anything else by then unless you went tae Copland and Lye's.'

'We haven't got the scene set yet,' the director said.

Belle passed a corner where bulldozers were nudging the gable and plaster dust was rising in a roar. The street-map was patched with gap-sites and bothies and builders' boards. 'Pat an Rose shoulda moved oot long ago,' she said. 'Pat shoulda got his act thegither. Got a job. Got a new hoose. In Wolfhill. Nae pubs.'

From the bulldozed streets rose the high flats, spectral in the mist. 'Helluva phallic,' said Belle. When the rosy haze cleared away they were windy and unfriendly and unprotected, a training ground for Tam Ratface and his pals. 'Nae fuckin chance he'da got his act thegither there,' she said.

The doors waited for her. Glass prisms in the Willow Tearoom. A woman turning into a tree. Spooky women and roses guarding the art school door.

'Can I go through that one?' Belle said. She'd thought of doing textile design. 'Mary Quant,' she explained. 'Minis.' Patrick Brady indicated there wasn't much textile there. It was Rose's legs he was looking at. 'But you've still tae get it right,' Belle said. Pat and Rose weren't listening to her.

Her father just looked at her with fish eyes. She persisted till a belting was on the horizon, and then she walked out. The careers woman riffled through leaflets, pink and green and blue. 'You've always been a great reader, haven't you? What about this instead?'

The door saying SILENCE was ready at hand. 'It isny right,' said Belle.

'But the arts couldn't get along without libraries,' the director solemnly said. 'They couldn't get along without you, Belle. Like a doctor without a nurse.'

'Like a husband without a wife,' the cameraman agreed.

'Like a fish withoot a fuckin bicycle,' said Belle, but they surrounded her and told her how sensible she was being, and everything went quiet and boring as they pushed her through the library door.

6

You'd think after all that they would be concentrating on then-Belle. 'Whit I'm lookin for,' she said, 'is that no the idea?' But it was quite a cosy scene they zoomed in on. Two red-haired lassies in their petticoats sitting on a bed. Belle was supposed to be experimenting with ways to do Rose's hair for her wedding, but what she was really doing was telling Rose all about this guy Cameron who'd started coming into the library. 'Kinna obvious whit I'm lookin for there, right enough,' now-Belle said.

'But it wasn't right,' the director said with a frown.

'Fuckin disaster zone, start tae feenish,' Belle agreed.

'Don't let's forget the question of why.'

'Why it wis a disaster? Shouldny have merriet him in the first place, that's fuckin why.'

'Why you did marry him,' the director sighed, faint yet pursuing. 'It was supposed to be the sexual revolution after all.'

'Well, I didny revolve.'

So there was Belle twisting Rose's hair up on plastic rollers, and the two dresses hanging on the wardrobe door, the white lace and the peach silk. 'See, there's this old village underneath the Central Station,' Belle said. 'Everybody kens it's there, it was in the *Sunday Post*. Built over but it's still there. Cobblestones, pavements, houses, shops. Names above the shop doors.'

'Would the trains no fall through?' said Rose.

'You'd wonder, wouldn't you,' said Belle, 'but naw, it's still there and you can get intae it. There's a door under the bridge. This guy Cameron telt me that. He knows a guy that knows a guy who's got a key.'

'Cameron?' Rose said, perking up.

'Comes in at lunchtimes. I wis lookin at a book about the village an we got talking about it. He says he'll take me down there.'

'Is he nice?'

'He's okay.'

'It'll be handy,' said Rose, 'you havin your own place. Pat an me had a terrible job – well – you know.'

But Belle didn't know what she was talking about. Not right away.

'How could you not know?' the cameraman was forced to object. 'That was why Rose was getting married for God's sake.'

'I didny. Okay?'

Right in his face, so he backed off and the director hastily began scribbling on her clipboard. 'See, this is hard to believe. *Knew Pat had got Rose into trouble. Didn't know how??* I suppose you'd been brought up not to think about it. John Knox,' offered the director triumphantly.

'Didny want tae think aboot it,' said Brady far away.

So when Belle did cotton on she went redder than her hair. 'I haveny taken Cameron home.'

'No yet,' said Rose.

'We never – He's never – He doesny –'

'Well, he will,' said Rose, 'an if he doesny, you chuck him, okay?'

Rose said that! Wee Rose! The innocent one! It was Belle who was always getting a smack round the face for looking at boys. But that was then, and now-Belle saw them both grow up in time-lapse photography, which solved one of the director's problems at least. Belle stretched from a gawky schoolgirl to a young library assistant, equally awkward, equally shy. Rose grew up in much more spectacular style, from a toddler to a long-legged lassie to an absolute smasher, with a lot of Belle in the line of her cheek and the turn of her head, but her hair was strawberry blonde. Behind her shoulder stood a shadowy little boy. 'John?' Belle uncertainly said.

Patrick Brady was always there or thereabouts. His dog Saigon was okay with Rose and Belle ('Makes mair fuss o that dug than he does o me,' Rose said), but never failed to growl at their father, who threatened to have it put down. Pat's five sisters kept him in order to some extent and raised hell if they smelt drink on his breath, but obviously they couldn't stop him smoking and standing on street corners whistling after girls, and that's how he spent most of his time.

The director started leafing back through her papers in a worried way. 'Fifties? Sixties? Wasn't there national service then? Shouldn't he have done that?'

'He coulda been a conchie,' offered Belle, 'but I'm no sure he had the brains.'

The researcher came galloping up with the info and the director sighed in relief. 'No, here we are. National service finished in 1960 and he'd only be fourteen then.' Her papers flew up, circled, settled like white moths under her hand. 'But he wouldn't have been taken anyway. Heart murmur as a child.'

Belle told them that was a load of crap.

There he was on the street corner, hanging about, whistling to Saigon, laughing when a girl looked round, ready and willing to take it from there. Six foot two. Quite the brick shithouse. Hung like a donkey. If we're talking heart murmurs it's the lassies are having them. And passing in the street with his clinking shopping-bags was Belle's father, a respectable man. Random binges. Now and then a red-eyed rage. Belle and Rose knew when to run for cover. 'If he lays a fuckin finger on Rose I'll fuckin swing for him,' Pat said with drink taken one night.

'The last hanging in Britain was in 1964,' the researcher felt she had to let them know.

Belle stared at Patrick and said 'Oh thanks a bunch.' That confused him. Easily done. He scowled at her under his black brows and muttered something or other. She could fuckin look after herself, that sort of thing. Meant to be a compliment, she supposed.

And so she could. She got the library job, got a bedsit, got out. Worked shifts, but you could read in the quiet times. She came across the story of the old village in a newspaper and found more about it in the local history section. She was reading a big old dusty book at the counter one lunchtime when Cameron came in. Now-Belle saw then-Belle, the bubbly red hair needing a good cut, the long legs and long fingers and the incongruous scholar's frown between her brows, and Cameron coming up to the counter, not very tall but dapper in his suit and polished shoes.

'Good book?' he enquired.

She started, made to shut the book, knocked a pile of request slips off the counter, went to pick them up all of a fluster, but Cameron was already doing the gentlemanly thing.

'Was that it?' demanded now-Belle in disgust.

'No quite.'

He looked at the book, still open at a street plan of the old village. Of course they talked about it. 'Seemingly it's still there,' said Belle, 'though I don't know why the trains don't fall through.'

Cameron didn't offer an opinion on that, but she never noticed because what he did say was so exciting. 'Oh, it's still there all right. Somebody I know, he's seen it. Told me he was down there just yesterday, walking about on the cobbles among the old houses and shops.'

'Couldny resist that. Who could?' said now-Belle. 'Mind you it was the best sentence he ever uttered in the whole o his fuckin life.'

'This chap's a friend of a friend,' said Cameron, 'says he'll take me down some time. Would you like to come?'

'And that was it, I suppose?'

'No quite,' then-Belle said.

There it was, the scene next time she went home. Rose pale and weepy, her father incandescent with rage, Patrick Brady nowhere to be seen. When she came to think, she'd heard about it on the bus, two sharp-voiced wives behind her, though she never imagined they were talking about Rose.

'Two months gone.'

'T-t-t.'

'No surprise mind you. Canny keep it in his troosers that boy.'

'They're aw the same. Think they've jist tae go tae confession an bob's yer uncle.'

'That'll no get him oot o it this time. Her faither's a decent man.'

Who threatened Rose with everything under the sun, but the trouble was she'd got her second wind, and what he threatened her with was exactly what she wanted to do anyway. 'Married to that scoundrel! A baby every year!'

'Maybe twins.' If she hadn't been pregnant she would definitely have got a thrashing for that, even Rose.

So Pat was found and interrogated and said that marrying Rose was absolutely jake by him. And so the wedding was fixed. ('You wouldny credit it, would you?' said now-Belle.) They even got a house, and Belle went up with them to scrub floors and hang curtains. Nice neighbours too, a quiet woman and a bouncy friendly red-headed man. 'Anything I can dae for you, just say,' he begged beautiful bright-haired Rose when they collided on the doorstep. Pat was two floors down struggling with a stepladder.

'Anither ginger top. Came in handy later on,' reflected now-Belle.

Did she start to push things a bit with Cameron then? Did he do the pushing? Was it just the wedding fever getting to them both? She remembered telling him all about it in a coffee-bar after work, so they must have got that far at least. The thing had been discovered in time to head off the worst of it, and so the wedding wasn't going to be any hole and corner affair, but a nuptial mass (with papal blessing), a white lace dress (with swagged front), and Belle on bridesmaid duty in peach silk.

'Peach silk? That will suit you,' Cameron said.

How did she manage to get him invited, since he wasn't even her official boyfriend and she was supposed to be paired off with the best man? She had an idea that the crunch came with the best man, who was five foot tall and about the same broad. Everybody knew he was going to get legless quite early on ('*He's* supposeta be lookin after *me?*' Pat said), and his wife would be there, pregnant with their third. Anyway there wasn't a big turn-out on Rose's side and she was delighted to write out a last-minute invitation for Cameron. 'I'll wear my kilt of course,' he promised. Now-Belle could still remember what Patrick remarked when she reported that.

But Rose was quite pleased, and it was Rose's day. Even the five sisters didn't manage to take it away from her, Philomena, Teresa, Bernadette, Mary Margaret and Josephine. No, Mary Margaret was a Carmelite by then. The others were all there with their husbands and squads of kids and they were okay. The best man managed to make a sort of speech. Belle had to have the first dance with him, and then, equally by custom and law, she had to dance the next with the groom.

'Cameron wis pawin the floor by then,' now-Belle said. He didn't know anybody but Belle, couldn't get to sit beside her, didn't speak the language, and all those nieces and nephews on the groom's side weren't helping his temper. Every now and then, when the music stopped, little voices lilting 'Kiltie, kiltie, cauld arse' could be heard all over the hall.

Pat was a good dancer. He'd served his time at the Plaza and the Locarno and even a bony big lassie like Belle with her long arms and two left feet managed to keep in step, dancing with him. In step. In tune. His dark hair had escaped from the Brylcreem and it fell over his eyes. She felt his heart beating. Nae fuckin murmur there.

'That was it,' said Belle.

''Fraid so,' the director agreed.

She danced with Cameron then. She wondered what he had in his pocket. ('No, that's the oldest joke in the world,' the director yelled, and

Belle said 'But I did.') In due course they waved Pat and Rose off on their honeymoon, which everybody knew was taking place on the big bed in their new house three floors up. The four brothers-in-law had been threatened with excommunication if they didn't leave them alone, and the neighbours would stuff cottonwool in their ears. ('Or maybe no,' said now-Belle.)

It began to be time for the party to break up. The best man, obviously, had to go home with his pregnant wife. Just as obviously it was up to Cameron to offer the bridesmaid a run home, not to her father's house of course, but to her own wee bedsit on the fringe of the west end. All student flats and rooms, nobody noticing or caring who you brought home. ('When I think o it,' said now-Belle, 'I coulda been shaggin the whole o the medical school.')

Obviously, Belle had to ask Cameron up for coffee. How obvious was it to him that he wasn't really the person she was asking up at all?

Perhaps not very. Perhaps he didn't care. He sat awkwardly on her slippery leatherette sofa while she pottered about with the kettle and the coffee-mugs. 'Suits you,' he said, 'the peach silk.' As the dressmaker had pointed out with some pride, it fitted like a glove over hips and bust, thanks to the long zip all the way down the back. Cameron came up behind Belle and pulled the long zip down and the peach silk cascaded like petals around her feet.

As did her tights, quite soon, if not in such romantic billows and puffs. And her pants, peach silk too, as Cameron approvingly observed. 'Matching accessories, that wis very him,' said Belle. It was hellish uncomfortable on the sofa, but, slithering about and yelping quite as much from pins and needles as from desire, they went all the way, there in Belle's bedsit while Pat and Rose enjoyed their papally blessed, absolutely legitimate wedding night, and the ginger-haired neighbour covered his ears, maybe, through the wall..

'And that's why I married him,' said Belle. 'You really fuckin wouldny believe it now.'

7

The director was in despair. Belle said irritably 'I telt you I hadny time tae swing. Plus Cameron needed a wife. The senior partner wis startin to gie him funny looks.'

They all thought about that for a while.

The voice-over man cleared his throat. 'Don't worry,' he said, and went into incantation mode. 'Two beautiful sisters and the prince who marries the wrong one. It is a classic story, a timeless tale.'

'Only if aw the characters concerned are total fuckin eedjits,' said Belle. 'But let's face it, most folk are.'

'Did Cameron ever take you to the village?' the director dared to enquire.

'Did he fuck.'

'Then maybe that's what you're looking for,' the cameraman said. He started discussing night-sights and emulsion, not the kind you put on walls.

But Belle was in the alley with Brady as she'd been before. In a dark alley with Pat Brady, who couldny keep it in his troosers, who'd served his time inside lassies' knickers! He was a stinking old wino with white bristles on his slabbery chin. 'How the fuck did that happen?' she said, and she could have cried.

'We know about him by now, Belle. It's you we're looking for.'

They were in the square courtyard with the barred windows and the green light from above, and the door with the peephole in the corner. Brady had collapsed beside it in a wheezing heap of rags and dirt. She stepped lightly up on to his bent knees, on to his shoulder, to look through the peephole. She weighed nothing at all. He didn't notice her, or if he noticed he didn't mind.

'Is it what you're looking for, Belle?' the director, the cameraman, the sound man, the voice-over man cried. She came down to earth as Brady roused and shook himself and farted and sneezed.

'I'm no sure.' Now beside her she saw the broken door, but she wasn't going there. 'Couldny reach it after aw. Couldny see,' she said, and they explained to each other, 'She can't see.'

'Disny want tae see,' Brady said.

Cameron said 'Friend of a friend. Take me down some time. Would you like to come?' and the director and cameraman just about wet themselves in their excitement. 'It's the village! We've found it! We must go in!'

'No yet,' Brady said. He was standing behind her and she was in front of the broken door.

'I'm no goin in there.'

'It won't make any difference if you do,' the director, busy with her clipboard, said.

'I haveny got the key.'

'Sure o that, are you?' Pat Brady said.

She touched the door with a fingertip. It began to open. He was at her back, pressing her on, so it didn't worry her that they were all crowding behind her, pushing her through the broken door.

They were all thudding downhill on a long steep ramp, faster and faster, down and round. They came out into an open space and their panting breath echoed in the corners of a roof. They couldn't go any farther because the way was blocked by a rubbish-tip. 'Everything bar the kitchen sink,' the cameraman observed, but the kitchen sink was there, with a swan-necked brass tap that Belle knew from a long time ago. She trembled and wept.

There was the west end bedstead with a pair of handcuffs casually clipped to one post. A hospital bed too. A pile of old doors heaped up for firewood. The junk and old iron rose more than head-high. Brady shrugged, took off his draggly coat and rolled it up ('No much room they've left us,') and pushed it ahead of him under the carcase of a Coronation tramcar. A wriggle and a kick took him out of sight.

The TV crew were through as well, though Belle didn't see them go. She stood alone in the darkness. 'I canny dae this,' she said.

'Sure aboot that, are ye?' said Brady from the other side.

She knelt down in the sharp rubble and wormed her way under the bedstead, where there seemed a little more room. No light ahead. She crawled two yards, knee and hand, hand and knee. She couldn't go on.

She was under the bed, and that was bad enough: old carpet-ends, a chipped chanty, dust in her mouth and throat, a rusty tin trunk threatening her shrinking skin. Through the wall her mother was crying. 'Pull yourself together, Agnes,' her father said. That was past, or it was ahead.

Here and now she lay under a bed in darkness and dust, and heavy on the bed the rubbish made an iron comforter, crazily crumpled high, ready to settle at a touch. Crushing and lightless above it the tunnel roof with its blocks of stone; and above the tunnel, pressing down, ancient storeys of deserted buildings, the whole weight of the street, of the city, of the world. All that held it up was the fragile rusty frame of the marriage bed, and it had collapsed long ago. She felt it breathe and stir. She scrabbled with toes and fingers and slid out with her nose on Brady's shitty broken shoes.

'Okay?' she heard him enquire as she gasped in the mud.

They still weren't in the village, they were in a passage, black as tar. Belle could see perfectly well, all the same, and the cameraman had his night-sight on. They pushed her on but she pulled back against their hands. 'This isny right. This isny what I'm looking for,' she said.

'It's on the way,' the director said.

The soundman looked doubtfully at his levels as Belle screamed 'You don't know! You don't need to know!' The director tried to say something else but Belle clapped her hands to her ears and didn't hear. 'It isny right so there's nae point being here,' she said.

'The thing is, Belle, we haven't set the scene yet,' the director patiently explained.

That wasn't easy, because hardly anybody remembered the foggy, sooty old city now. Black tenements reared up, but they were only ghosts. Nobody believed in them so they didn't stay. The voice-over man intoned statistics about TB. Mass X-rays. Didn't help Patrick's cousin Maggie Mullen, who died before she was twelve.

Third week of November, depend on it, fog. It got in past the window-sashes, down the area steps, in through the brass letter-box, with its deep silence and its own smell.

'Open fires of course,' the director said. They tried a coal-lorry drawn by a huge patient horse, and they tried the corner shops with their bundles of kindling for sale. Quick fingers, blue with cold, built a fire in the iron grate, and that worked. Belle remembered that.

She circled the house, floating in the air. A nice house, a good-class tenement, red sandstone, tiled close. Not like the tenements farther down the hill where the trams rattled and clanged. Belle got the sour whiff of beer and spirits, clear as if she was walking past a pub, and there was a pub for every three houses down there.

The broken door was there. It had been broken long ago. It hung from one hinge and the smell of strong soap and hot water came out. She touched it with a finger. It opened a crack. The shadows were wrong. A swinging shadow that she didn't want to see.

'I canny. I'm no goin,' she said.

'You canny stop, Belle,' said Brady, 'now you know there's somethin there.'

'Go in the front door like a civilised being,' her aunt said.

'I haveny got the key. I'm no allowed a key.'

An old smooth yale key appeared in her hand. She put it in the lock, and turned it, and took hold of the polished brass handle, and walked in.

Her mother was ironing in the kitchen. Steamy warmth from the blanket-covered board and dry red heat from the sleepy fire in the range. The wireless playing and her mother humming along. 'There you are, wee one,' she said. Belle saw her clearly at last, her curly brown hair pinned up out of the way, the smile in her hazel eyes. It was worth it, the whole thing, just for that.

Then the kitchen was empty and cold. 'Don't tell Belle,' they said. 'She doesn't need to know.'

8

Fog of course. Belle blew her nose on a clean hanky and folded the smear of greasy dirt away. No TV crew recorded her doing that. Nobody had TV then. Well, Patrick Brady's rackety family did, and where they got the money you shuddered to think.

All neat and tidy, Belle and Rose and their mother and father, going to church, quarter to eleven, just nice time to get in and nod to friends and sit back. In a douce procession of churchgoers strung out along the street, who didn't know that Belle's father had chased her round the house with his razor strop because she couldn't find her Bible. Sundays didn't play well with him. And he caught her too.

Brady sloped past them with his fox's grin. He went to church at all sorts of funny times. And in August he went back to school a week before Belle because they got funny days off. When he did go to church, or to school.

'Who's that?' Belle's father barked.

'Margaret's cousin Patrick.'

'Who's Margaret? Where did you meet her?'

'Margaret Mullen from dancing class. She came to my birthday party.'

'Agnes, you mustn't let her bring just anybody home.'

'Why?' Belle said, and knew when his eyes bulged like gooseberries that she shouldn't have said that..

Out in the foggy streets where the trams clanged their bells. Down into the Merchant City, though nobody called it that. 'Wait here,' her father said. 'Little girls can't come in here.'

'Why not? It's only a bank.' Her mother laughed at that. Her father wasn't pleased. Her mother pulled a face behind his back. 'Us girls, we have to look after each other,' she said. Rose was too wee, just starting to toddle about on her reins, so that meant Belle.

They sat round the fire in the kitchen with the wireless playing dance music, not loud enough to disturb Belle's father reading his book. Her mother did a dance step or two at the ironing board, but her father barked 'The girl's doing her homework, Agnes,' and Belle knew not to look. Her mother knew not to dance and the pile of ironed shirts grew. Her father stubbed out his fag on the shiny bars of the grate. 'Bedtime for little girls,' he said.

Her mother wasn't well and they wouldn't say what was wrong. Their stiff aunt came to look after Belle and Rose. Then it was sort of explained. It was because of John. 'That makes mammies tired,' her aunt said. Belle looked down at him in his cot but all you could see was a fluff of red hair. Rose was so small she couldn't see into the cot, cried, had a tantrum, got a skelp.

A milky smell off the cot. Sometimes a not very nice smell. 'Did you not notice, Agnes?' her aunt said, coming in with hot water and clean things. 'I can't stay for ever, you know. I've got my own house to attend to. You'll have to get up tomorrow. You'd have been as well to wait till this one was off your hands,' because Rose had fallen and bumped her head again.

'He was awful keen to have a boy,' her mother's tired voice said. 'When he saw Rose he said "Another lassie?" That was all he said.'

Her mother didn't get up. Didn't get well. Clinking and flapping noises from the big bedroom, and when the door was opened a smell like fog. A damp sick smell. When she was allowed in her mother was crying. 'You'll frighten the child, Agnes,' her father said.

'The thing is,' Belle said, 'I canny remember why I was under the bed.'

'Badminton rackets,' Brady said. 'Maggie had one but the strings was broke. Under the bed wi the other junk, you thought, mind?'

Bits of carpet and abandoned dolls and the *Children's Encyclopedia* and a tin trunk. Belle couldn't see any badminton rackets there and she crawled farther in. The back wall of her room was the side wall of the big bedroom. Her mother was still crying. 'Pull yourself together, Agnes,' her father said.

'I can't. I can't.'

'Of course you can. What's wrong with you?'

'I don't know.' Weeping and crying sore.

Belle knew she could make it better. Look after her. Give her a hug. Tell her not to cry. She began to back out and cracked her ankle-bone on the tin trunk. Got stuck. Couldn't get out. Started to cry. When she finally got out, all dirty and snottery, her father was coming out of the bedroom. 'Your mother's trying to sleep,' he said. 'Don't disturb her. No, Belle, do as I say.' And her aunt came out of the kitchen and gave her a skelp because she'd got cobwebs all over her school skirt.

'But it was another day,' Belle said. 'Another day.'

'You know whaur you're gaun, Belle,' Pat Brady said.

'Where's my mammy?' she said. It was cold early spring. The kitchen smelled of cabbage and bleach. 'I found a beetle in this kitchen. A beetle! Run away and don't bother me,' the stiff aunt said.

'Where is she?' She looked in the best room and the bathroom and the hall cupboard, just in case. Greatly daring, she looked in the big bedroom, but her mother wasn't there, though the damp sick smell was there, the smell of tears. The cot was quiet. She came back to the kitchen and looked out into the grey back green. 'She's in the washhouse,' she said.

'Tut, Belle, why would she be there?'

'That's where she is.' Belle wrestled open the back door and ran along the flagstone path.

'Why would she –' Her aunt's voice cut off as if she had been shot.

Running footsteps on the flagstones, Belle's and her aunt's, who'd never been known to run. The washhouse smelled of soap and hot water, though it was never used now. The broken door hung from one hinge. Belle tried to push it open but it wouldn't budge. Something had fallen over, jamming the door.

'No, Belle, go back to the house.' Her aunt was tall enough to see through the crack at the top of the door. What had she seen? Maybe a shadow in the wrong place. 'Go back and look after the baby.' And she stopped. 'Oh God, the baby,' she said, and Belle had never heard her swear.

'I went in under the bed again,' Belle said in a chatty way. 'They couldny get me oot for two days. Ma faither yanked me oot an gied me a leatherin on ma bare bum because I'd peed the lino.'

In the park, under the new young leaves and the foaming pear-blossom, she stood on a red marble bridge. The little river crawled below, soiled with waste and spill. Pat Brady looked at her with big dark eyes in a wee triangular face. 'Though you'd flitted,' he said.

'Rose an me went to my auntie's for a while.'

'You're back now.'

'Aye.'

He didn't say any more. A thin black dog came up and nudged his elbow. 'This is Yang,' he said. 'Short for Pyongyang.'

'Funny name for a dog,' Belle listlessly said.

'Fancied the sound o it,' said Patrick. 'An see, when I say it he wags his tail.' He knelt down and lifted up Yang's right forepaw. 'He's learnt tae shake hands,' he said. 'Shake hands wi Belle, c'mon, ya stupid cunt.'

Belle shook hands with Yang. The rough pads, something she'd never felt before, warm and real.

9

The TV crew were camped in the park bandstand, trying out angles and cuts, zooming in on the heartbreaking young green of the trees. 'Naw, that's no right,' said Belle. 'Naebody had TV then.'

'Rewind,' said Brady to the director, who did as she was told. Back at speed from the park to the funeral. Belle and Rose in their Sunday best. A brown coffin and a tiny white coffin and their aunt's grey shattered face. 'Never the same efter that,' Belle observed. 'Turned up at ma weddin an tried tae pinch the sundae spoons.' What her father looked like she couldn't see.

And the camera pulled back. She still couldn't see what had happened in the washhouse, but for the first time she saw herself, then-Belle, under the bed. Crouched among the broken dolls and carpet-ends, fairisle jumper and school skirt, ankle socks, scuffed shoes. A frightened wee lassie with her mother weeping next door.

'Now I go in,' she said. 'Tell her no tae cry.' But that wasn't on the director's clipboard, and in fact they'd even lost the washhouse door. Beside them was the very old door with the peephole. Just that alone. She couldn't quite reach the peephole after all. The answer of course was to float in the air and then it would be easy to look through, but something was holding her down and she couldn't do that. It was the dog Yang or maybe Kuwait, sitting on her feet, looking up into her face adoringly, the way he only looked at Pat.

So she opened the door and they all went in. It wasn't the village, it was another bit of passage, that was all, glimmering with green light from a grating, strong wooden joists holding up the high roof. 'Nothing here,' the director said.

Brady kicked the debris of a hundred years off smooth old cobblestones. He crooked his finger at what could have been the edge of a pavement, running for a few yards and disappearing into a wall. The cameraman filmed it without enthusiasm. Dark chunks on the cobbles that could have been turds or coal. A slab of wood thick as a windowsill. A flat board lettered with what could just have been a name. 'There's naethin here an it's no whit I'm lookin for,' Belle said.

'There's a problem with the light, love,' fretted the director.

'I didn't expect to be filming fucking badgers.' The cameraman scrabbled and rooted in his box of delights.

'Roon the corner,' said Brady, out of sight, far away. They followed his voice. 'Holy God,' the cameraman said.

'We've found it! This is it!' the director cried.

'Naw, it's no.' But they weren't listening to Belle.

The researcher spooled out yards of notes which the director grabbed and passed to the voice-over man. 'The village of Grahamston, the site of which is almost entirely occupied by the Central Station, extended from Argyle Street to Gordon Street and from Union Street to Hope Street. It boasted only one street, Alston Street, running north to south.' And there the one street was. The camera followed it all along its length. 'Camera tricks,' said Belle.

'Residents in 1865,' the voice-over man intoned. 'McEwan, Jas B, teacher of dancing. Boyle, Mrs William, contractor. Geddes, Robert, and Sons, merchants. Spalding, Mrs, ladies' nurse.'

Belle felt the hard cobblestones under her soles, smoothed by feet and wheels. The doorways and shop-fronts stood where they ought to be; she saw the arches leading farther in. 'Jesus,' she said. 'It's took half a fuckin lifetime but here I am. Here we are.'

Blue light. The camera steadied and rose. A vaulted roof above the cobbled street, the flat flags of a pavement, the moulding round a front door. A shop window with gilded lettering above. Belle smelled bacon and firelighters and dry tea and cats.

'Get as much as you can, love,' the director cried. 'Here's a fireplace. Here's a cupboard. Oh God, there's an old bottle, let's have the label, clear as you like. Oh Lord! Hooks in the ceiling here! A butcher's, yah?' Up the long street with the rumble of trains overhead. 'We can't be far from the surface,' the director said, 'I can hear voices,' and so could Belle.

She was carried along with the TV crew. Camera angles swooping, veering, poking into hidden things. Shadows melted and ran ahead of the lights, and the shadows weren't as empty as they should be. Definitely somebody there. Pat Brady stepped out on to the cobbled street in front of the director and the cameraman and the soundman and the voice-over guy. He stretched out his hands and shoved them and they folded up like paper flowers. They were gone.

'You have the power!' said Belle.

'Naw, Belle, that's you.'

He grinned at her, a black-haired boy. 'Patrick,' she said, 'I don't know where I'm going.'

'Aye you do.'

Here after all, the old village. She walked on its cobbles under an ancient moon. Under all the layers it was here, the old quiet street, grocer and bootmaker and gunmaker and spirit-dealer and chimney-sweep, black leaning storeys above. Geddes the merchant and Mrs Spalding the ladies' nurse and Jamesie McEwan the dancing teacher; she heard their voices, though they weren't quite to be seen. And Mrs Boyle, contractor. You go, girl. 'You been here since eighteen sixty-five?' she enquired. The researcher corrected 'Eighteen seventy-nine. Central Station opened. They'd all be gone by then.' No answer from the ghosts in their other world.

'Get on wi't!' shouted Mrs Boyle, so loud you could hardly hear Geddes gossiping across the street. 'And one, two, three,' chirped Jamesie, but Mrs Spalding pushed him aside. 'How are we today? You'll need to be getting your strength up. A nice drop of soup,' she said.

The clop and rattle of an underground stream crossed the path. 'There are many rivers,' Cameron explained, though far away. 'Still there. Like the village. The Anderston Burn and the Finnieston Burn. The Pinkston Burn and the Poldrait Burn.'

'The Girth Burn and the Blind Burn,' chimed in Geddes, and 'Jenny's Burn. The Nameless Burn. The Reidclaith Gott,' chanted Mrs Boyle, who probably had customers on the banks of those lost streams.

'The Molendinar,' Belle said, throwing a pebble or a turd into the stream.

'No, no, that's quite across the city,' Cameron scolded, 'this is the St Enoch Burn,' but it was the Molendinar running at Belle's feet, all the way from long ago. Tin cans and toilet paper. Dirty where it should run clean. Cameron paid no notice and went ahead with his roll-call of rivers. She wondered if, like the other people in the place, she wasn't there.

She went farther in. Down and down and down. Farther below.

All the dogs ran ahead of her, Kuwait and Derry and Kabul and Saigon and Yang, and Brady was hunkered down beside a little smudge fire. The red light showed his black hair and dark eyes. No, his greasy old bunnet and the white bristles on his chin. The voices were silent, though Belle couldn't say where the people had gone. Far, far inside, when she cupped her hands round her ears, she caught maybe just the echo of padding feet, going on and down and down. She had this mad picture of Pat and Rose's house three stairs up, exactly as it used to be but turned on its head, deep below the ground.

And everything upside down. Or the right way up at last.

'Shops an houses, an they built the Central Station on top,' she said.

'Ah, it's like the buggers,' said Brady, 'they wouldny care.'

He hawked and spat into the fire, and she hated that. 'Patrick, that's a fuckin dirty thing tae do.'

'Jesus, you're as bad as Bernadette,' he said.

He took his bunnet off and it wasn't that bad. In the veils of smoke twisting up from the living fire the shop-fronts weren't so clear and neither was he, but there was a look in his eye. She hunted through her pockets for the triangle of mirror she combed her hair in. A flame spurted up and she got a glimpse of bubbly red curls. Really she knew it was dry and grey and cut as short as a punk's to keep the nits under control.

'We're no as young as we wis, Belle,' Patrick said in the dark.

She said automatically, 'Ah, there's life in you yet.' So there was. A look in his dark eye.

'I feel whiles,' said Brady, 'there's too much.'

The flame had died. The mirror was black and dead. Only their voices breathing in the vault. 'I know the feelin,' she said.

'An there's no much tae be done aboot it,' said Brady. 'No at my age. The way I've let mysel go.' He choked on phlegm or tears. 'Mother o God, Belle, who'd hae me?'

'Who have you asked?' she said.

And when they took their clothes off they were both twenty-three years old. Funny that.

Brady fell asleep afterwards, snorting and whistling in a litter of coats. 'Ah God, exhausted frae his labours,' said Belle, and pulled his old jacket up to cover his goosepimpled lanky bare arm. His face was as grey as the cobblestones, but a good sleep would get his strength up. There was a wide red-marble bridge that she knew but didn't know. Beyond the green trees a tramcar rattled by, and the high glass towers took fire from the rising sun.

10

Camera tricks. Three statues of women in the whole city, Queen Victoria (of course) and some do-gooder in Govan and La Pasionara by the grey river shaking her fist at the sky. The escalator portraits, no women at all. Warehouses and banks looming in majesty because they'd been taken from ground level where ordinary people belonged. Bills addressed to her father, and her father writing cheques. Cameron carrying out the very same weighty work, what a husband had to do. ('If naethin else,' said Belle.) John Knox high on his pillar above the city and its graves. 'We canny get away from him, can we?' said Belle.

The director nodded absently and went on shuffling her scene-setting shots into place. Film was being cut up and spliced. The voice-over man had packed up and gone away, good riddance. 'Put me in mind o Cameron,' Belle said.

'Hmm. I think it's time for a run-through,' the director said. Cameron nodded eagerly and said 'The rushes,' to show how much he knew, though from the director's expression Belle suspected that wasn't a lot. 'It's not edited. Still a bit impressionistic. We might keep it like that,' the director said.

So it was a quick reprise of the cathedral, Belle in white satin and tulle, John Knox in the pulpit, Patrick complaining about his bum. And on to the west end house. 'Still far too long,' the director said. In a way Belle didn't mind. Forget the boring days and the sad desperate nights. There's the scene of Pat laughing in his kitchen because Rose is expecting again. 'Keep that, okay?' said Belle.

Then the wasteground with Belle washing herself in the cold dawn. A night scene she hadn't noticed them filming, with Brady snuffling and snoring, and Tam Ratface humping Lizzie, and car headlights swinging over the rubble, breaking into glitter on hills of broken glass. Then back, all out of sequence, to the good red sandstone tenement, well away from those Catholic families down the hill. 'Margaret Mullen's cousin Patrick has five sisters,' Belle said. Her father wasn't at all surprised.

And back to the churchgoers, mother, father, two wee girls. Another lassie? What a shame. But there's time yet. And back to Belle getting her school skirt filthy in the dust under the bed. Her mother in the next room, crying sore.

'Now I go in and gie her a hug. Tell her no to cry. Tell her I love her.

Show us that,' said Belle with the tears running down her face. But the director didn't. Couldn't. 'Not possible, Belle,' she said, 'because it didn't happen, you see.'

'Fuckin useless director you are,' Brady said.

They were on the red marble bridge again with all the dogs, Kuwait, Kabul, Derry, Saigon and Yang, frisking round their feet. Belle was a wee girl in a school skirt, and a trollopy old bag lady, and a red-haired lassie with long legs. Brady was a raggedy wee boy and a smelly pile of shit and a big fellow needing a haircut, but the dark eyes were the same. 'I'm awful, awful sorry, Belle,' he said. As he couldn't have said then.

'It was my fault. Should've looked after her. My fault.' As she couldn't ever have said.

'No your fault, Belle. You couldny dae a fuckin thing. I've been tellin you. You couldny. No there, no then.'

Now-Belle looked at then-Belle, a wee lassie in a world made for her father and John Knox. At her mother in that same world. 'That's right. I couldny,' she said. All her bones were melting and relaxing in a great sad relief. In their centre, a point of light. She stepped forward to give her mother a hug.

And the park was fading. The red tenement was nearly gone. The old guys on the wasteground piped like crickets. They were too long or too narrow under their blankets, against the warehouse walls that were lacy as winter leaves.

Belle looked at her own hands, strong and thin, three-dimensional against the fading trees. She could feel Yang's warm rough paw in hers, though the foggy city was long gone. She could feel Brady at her back, hard and young. When she turned round there he was, twenty-three, with that fuck-you grin. Then he wasn't there, but she knew what she was looking for now.

Swing doors in front of her. THE CLEMENT ATTLEE WARD. She pushed them open and went in.

The fireworks were still going off and she was still in bed. She could see the rockets in the midnight sky, even though the window was behind her head. Rockets to the moon and busy banging clusters of sparkles and great opening umbrellas of stars, red and gold and green and silver and blue.

She had been washed. She was clean. They were all propped up in bed, neat and tidy, because it was visiting time. The gentle Irish nurse saw her looking at the door and smiled. 'Expecting somebody, Belle?'

'She doesn't need to know,' the hard young voice decreed.

He'll no like to come in, she thought. He'll think he's no allowed. An then there's the dug. She reached into her locker for her plastic bag of clothes. Shrugged into her coat, which they'd let her keep since she didn't have a dressing-gown. 'Gaun tae the loo,' she said hardily to any nurse she met, and they crumpled up and faded away. She went straight on, through the swing doors.

The station was just on the other side of the doors. She saw Tam Ratface sloping off into the gents, and she saw Lizzie touting her wares, and she saw Cameron buying a porn magazine at the kiosk. She sat down on a red plastic bench and got dressed. Nobody noticed. Brady wasn't there. 'Still in his scratcher. Laziest bugger in God's creation. Bernadette wis never done yellin aboot that. Rose didny seem tae mind,' she said.

But Kuwait's cold nose nuzzled her hand and she knew Brady was somewhere near. She looked around the big empty station concourse that floated and rocked in the pearly mist, and all the dogs came racing across it and gathered round her feet. All the dogs of Brady's life, Kuwait and Kabul and Derry and Saigon and Yang.

Machinery

September

Moved in. Seems a nice enough flat. At least it's quiet. Thank goodness. I had a bad time in my last place.

The landlady ushered me in as if it was Blenheim Palace, though it's only one bedroom, sitting-room, usual offices. I hadn't asked half the questions I wanted to before she said 'Must go, collect children, you know –' and slapped the keys down on the kitchen worktop and shot off. That's all I'll see of her except on rent day, I suppose. She's a young thing. Her and her husband, nothing in their mind but money. They're all the same.

She's given me a year's lease. It's good to feel safe.

Phoned cousin Bella to give her my new address. 'Main-door flat?' she says as if she'd never lived in Glasgow. Too high and mighty to know about Glasgow tenements now.

I explained. Eight flats in the close. You do remember what a close is, I suppose? A common stair? Tenement? Red sandstone, four storeys, tiled close?

'Didn't you like the high flats then?' she said.

'It wasn't a success,' I said, and hurried on. I haven't got time to waste on chit-chat, if she has.

This time I insisted on the main-door flat, and I told her that. It's the best, as long as the locks are secure. I made the landlady check them all. Bolts on the outside doors.

So I've got a proper front door, a bit of garden, a hedge and a gate, as I explained to Bella, but I've also got a door opening into the close. I can visit people in the other flats without going outside. 'Do you know anybody in the other flats?' Bella said. Silly question, just the sort she asks.

Otherwise she didn't seem very interested. Said she'd have to go. Tommy just in from work, something on stove, going to burn, she'd phone me back.

She hasn't so far.

It's the holiday weekend so there's nobody about on the stair. People away seeing their families, I suppose.

Out sweeping the close, very dirty, people don't bother nowadays, I don't think it's been swept for weeks.

The close door banged, it needs its spring renewed, and a woman came in, dropping her keys, scuffling to pick them up, getting dirt under her fingernails I should think. She jumped when she saw me at my door and dropped them again. She said a swear word and laughed. Nothing to laugh about, I'd say.

'Oh hello,' she said. 'You must be – ' She knew perfectly well who I was, she could see my name on the door. I said 'Jenny Jackson,' and she said 'Oh hi, I'm Esther.' Fancy name. 'I'm above you. Next floor up.'

'I hope you don't play loud music,' I said.

She said 'Er, no, just the usual.' I've heard that before.

Middle-aged. Loose jacket done up on the wrong buttons. Briefcase under her arm, or maybe one of those computer things. Bohemian rather than smart, I'd say.

'Come in,' I said. She hesitated but said all right. People are often a bit stand-offish at first.

I led her into the sitting-room. I'd quite forgotten that yesterday's paper was lying on the coffee-table. I like to get a paper in case. To make sure.

'Sorry,' I said, and whisked it away. 'Untidy. I'm still settling in.'

'Don't worry,' she said, 'mine's like this all the time. On a good day.' I don't think I'd boast about it, in her place.

She hoped I'd like it here. Nice area. That sort of thing.

'Nobody but me seems to clean the close,' I said.

'The flat across from you is empty just now,' Esther said. 'I'm sure the new people will see to it when they move in.' Not very helpful, I must say.

We sat down on the sofa and she smiled at me as if she wasn't sure where to go from there. I wanted to put her at her ease. 'Have you had much trouble with the landlady?' I said.

'Ah – ' Esther said. 'I'm an owner-occupier, actually.'

'You're lucky.' I started telling her about my late husband, how he lost all my money on the horses, but she looked uncomfortable and so I didn't go much beyond 1970, though there was plenty more to tell. 'So it's rented flats for me,' I said, 'and landladies bleed you dry. You wouldn't believe how much she charges. Extortionate really. For a place like this.'

'Um, I thought it was quite nice,' she said, looking round, 'but I suppose –'

'She runs a Mercedes and her husband has a Jag. That isn't right, is it?'

'I wouldn't know,' said Esther, rather shortly, it seemed to me. .

'And her temper is atrocious. I've never heard the like. She yells and swears at me. Effs and bees all the time.'

Esther looked at me. Definitely a bit cool now. 'I have met her,' she said. 'She comes round occasionally to check on things, I've met her in the close. She's never yelled at me.'

Does she think I'm a liar or what? Tears came into my eyes. I couldn't help it. I never can. 'You don't know the half of it,' I said. I had plenty to tell her. I told her everything.

Esther was fidgeting, trying to move, but she was in the corner of the sofa and I didn't let her out. 'Don't worry. It's always stressful moving house,' she was saying, and she managed to get up at last. 'Must go,' and off she went. I heard her opening her door upstairs, saying hello.

A man's voice answered. Younger than her, for she's no spring chicken. Who would that be then?

I expect they're talking about me.

I shut my door and I heard it. Thump, thump, thump. All around. Just the same as it was in my last place, in the high flats. The boys upstairs eventually moved out but the new people were just as bad. I hope I'm not going to be unlucky again.

Met Esther again in the close. 'Oh hello,' she said. At least she remembers who I am. She was going to walk past but I stopped her. I put my hand on her arm. Something important to say.

'There's a constant thumping noise,' I said, 'keeping me awake at night. Day and night in fact. I don't know where it's coming from.' I stared into her face. I did know, of course, but I was giving her a chance to own up.

Esther frowned, letting on she was surprised. 'I've never noticed it,' she said.

'All day and all night,' I said. 'Have you got any machinery on in your flat?'

'Machinery?' said Esther. 'No.'

'A central heating boiler maybe?'

'I don't have central heating.' Really, she couldn't be less helpful if she tried.

'Fridge? Washing machine?'

'The fridge isn't very noisy,' said Esther. 'Doesn't keep us awake so I can't believe it would bother you. Mind you, it would take a volcanic eruption to wake Sam.' She laughed. Would you believe it? As if it was a joke.

'Then it's your washing machine.'

She looked doubtful. That's it! I've tracked it down!

'It's not exactly young. I suppose it does jump about a bit in the spin cycle,' she said. 'But that only takes a couple of minutes and you said all day?' She paused. 'And all night? I never run it at night.' She was laughing again. Cheeky bitch. 'I've lived in a tenement for twenty years,' she said. 'I know how sound travels. Washing machines at night, no way.'

'What else would it be then?' I shouted.

She looked at me oddly. 'Have you noticed we're on a main road?' she said. 'Traffic maybe?'

'No. Not traffic,' I said. And I went indoors.

Now autumn's coming on it's cold and unwelcoming in the close. Stuffy, somehow, as if we were underground.

I'm still hearing the machinery. I thought it would be peaceful here. I've tried earplugs. Thump, thump, thump. Mark my words, it's a washing machine.

October

The back door to the close was open again. People will insist on leaving it open in the middle of the day. Don't they know about urban foxes? So far I've just glared. Quite often people glare back.

This time I had to say something. It was a fair-haired young man and when I told him off he looked surprised. 'I've only been out to the bins,' he said. 'Thirty seconds? And I did check for burglars first, honest I did.'

I think he's Esther's son. Same know-it-all air. A student no doubt. We're paying for him to insult his elders and betters.

'Foxes could get in,' I informed him.

He looked at me rather carefully. 'I don't think you should worry too much about that. Foxes tend to be nocturnal, on the whole,' he said.

I went indoors before he gave me any more cheek.

And the thumping went on.

I've been very patient. I've held off as long as I could. In the middle of the afternoon I couldn't stand it any longer. I went to Esther's door. She opened it, blinking as if she'd just wakened up. A biro in her hand and it was leaking ink everywhere. 'You've got machinery on,' I said.

'Er, no,' she said. 'I'm writing. By hand.' She waved her messy biro, as if that proved anything at all.

But I knew better. 'I'm tired of this,' I said. 'Twenty-four hours a day, thump, thump, thump. You're running an illegal laundry.'

'What?' said Esther, laughing as if she couldn't believe her ears.

Laughing! I think she's mentally disturbed. Writers often are. 'An illegal laundry,' I said, slowly so she'd understand.

'No. I'm a writer. That's what I do.'

'An illegal laundry and I've got witnesses,' I said.

Esther gaped at me. After a minute she said, 'Jenny –' She paused and started again. 'Here you are standing on my doorstep. The door's open. Can you hear anything at all in this flat?'

'You've turned it off,' I said.

While she sought for an answer, I demanded to see her kitchen, where the washing machines are.

'I don't know – ' said Esther, looking startled. Behind her in the flat I heard her son say something very rude.

She turned away and he spoke again. She turned back and said 'Sam doesn't like that idea, and I agree.'

'That proves it!' I cried. 'If you were innocent you'd let me in!'

Esther sighed. 'This is too ridiculous,' she said.

'Let me in!'

Those quiet people, you can't trust them. 'I'm not letting you in,' she said. 'Look, the first time I met you? You went on for an hour, one hour by the clock, about your landlady. And neighbours you used to have.'

'It was all true,' I said.

'Well, maybe,' she said. 'It's just that I don't want to know what you would say about me.'

'Are you calling me a gossip?' I demanded.

'Oh hell,' she said, staring at me. I don't think there was any need for that sort of language.

After a bit she said, 'Look, I'm not running a laundry. I am the last person in the universe who would conceivably be found running a laundry. Or could run a laundry, come to that. I'm a writer. We're often not very good at running laundries.'

'Oh, I know all about you, Esther,' I said.

Esther said 'Go away, you silly old bat,' and shut the door.

I phoned the landlady and complained. Well, wouldn't you?

6.30 a.m. I couldn't sleep for the thumping. I went out into the back green and peered up at the windows to see who was operating machinery. Esther's kitchen window was brightly lit. The laundry was at work.

Later I met her in the close. Before I could say a word she was nattering on.

'Look, I'm sorry about yesterday. Sam told me I was pretty rude to you. The thing is, I was writing.' She was laughing again, a bit ashamed. As well she might be. 'Fortunately I was only making notes. If I'd been in the middle of a novel I'd probably have thrown you downstairs.'

I said: 'Are you threatening me?'

'Er,' said Esther. 'No.'

'Because you were in your kitchen at 6.30 this morning. Operating machinery. I saw your light on.' And as she hesitated: 'You can't deny it, can you?' I cried.

Esther took a deep breath. 'Clocks went back this morning,' she said. 'I woke early. Got up and made myself a cup of coffee. Took it back to bed. All right?'

'No, it is not all right,' I said. 'I know about your laundry business. Day and night. Thump, thump, thump. I'm going to tell the authorities.'

Eleanor looked at me strangely. 'I've told all my friends about my laundry business,' she said. 'They laughed like drains. They said if only they'd known they would have brought their washing round.'

'It's not funny!' I yelled.

'Have you considered tinnitus?' she was saying as I slammed my door.

November

Thump, thump, thump. At two a.m. it was too much for me. I came out on to the stair by my close door and went up to the first floor. Her storm door was shut. Trying to pretend nothing's going on.

I rang her doorbell. It's quite loud but I rang it again and again. She's not getting to make the excuse she didn't hear.

There was a scuffling and I saw a line of light through the crack of the storm door, where the two halves meet. That meant she'd opened her inside door. She was looking through the peephole in the storm door. 'Who is it?' she said in a scared voice. Serve her right if she's scared.

I didn't say anything.

'It's all right,' I heard her say, to her son I suppose. 'Not fire or police.' She murmured something I couldn't make out.

'What the hell?' her son said, only it wasn't 'hell'.

She murmured again.

'Well, put on your dressing-gown,' he said, 'you'll get cold.' I went on ringing and banging on the door while she was doing that.

Eventually she came back. She didn't open the storm door, so we were talking through solid wood. Frightened to face me, I suppose. 'Jenny,' she said, 'what on earth are you doing there at this time of night? It's after midnight.' (I heard her son behind her say 'It's after two,' with a very bad word in there.)'

I realised she could see me through her peephole, though I couldn't see her. Invisible. Threatening me.

I was brave and said, 'Have you any idea how much noise you're making there with your machinery?'

There was a pause, as if she didn't know how to answer. 'What are you talking about, Jenny? There's no machinery here,' she said.

'Oh yes!' I cried. 'I asked the man next door and he says it's coming from this flat!' I was quite pleased I'd thought of that. 'It's kept me awake for five weeks!'

'There's nothing here,' Esther said. 'We were asleep. You've woken us up. It's two in the morning, Jenny.'

'I'm going to call the authorities and have it monitored!' I said.

'Do that,' said Esther. 'Please. But for God's sake go back to bed just now and let us get back to sleep.'

'You're not going to get away with this!'

I heard the son say something like 'Let me –' and Esther saying 'Oh, leave it, no need to –' The inside door closed.

The glimmer from their hall lamp went out. I stood for a few minutes more on the silent landing under the sputtering stairlight. It's cold and frightening in the close at night. Like long ago. And the noise going on.

The shelter under the stairs. It was only a bare bulb and it kept blowing. Then it was pitch black and the next-door baby cried all the time. Thump, thump, in the sky.

In the morning I phoned the landlady. 'Oh yes, Jenny,' she said. 'I've had your neighbour on already to complain.'

'Complain?' I said. 'What has she got to complain about?'

It all reminded me of the high flats. Those boys were never done complaining. They moved out eventually. Good riddance, I said to their neighbour. 'They were nice boys,' she said, and looked oddly at me.

It seemed safe enough to go out. The noise, thump thump, but it was daylight and people were about. I went to the corner shop for a pint of milk. I passed the couple in the next main-door flat, pottering about in their garden, clipping and sorting things for winter. It's going to be nice here over the winter. Or it will be if I can get rid of the noise.

The next-door woman looked up and nodded to me. She looks like a quiet person who wouldn't stand for this nonsense. She'd take my side. 'What are we going to do about Esther?' I said.

She looked a bit surprised. 'You must be Jenny,' she said. 'Esther told me, um, she told me –'

'I daresay she made excuses,' I said.

'Well, I've known her for twenty years,' she said. 'No illegal laundry business in evidence during that time, I have to say.'

Her husband cleared his throat. 'So,' he said. 'Nice here, isn't it? How's the flat? Getting settled in?'

Cheeky, I'd call that. 'I've lived here for many years,' I said.

'Oh yes?' he said. There didn't seem to be much more that the two of them wanted to talk about. Probably they're in on her game.

It's no better. Thump, thump, thump. I put up with it as long as I could. I smoked half a packet, right down to the filters. No use.

I was shaking with nerves but I went up to her door. 'I want to come in and talk to you,' I said.

'Look –' Esther said. 'I'm working. I've just sat down at the computer. What is it about?'

'I must talk to you.'

'So talk,' said Esther rudely.

'You know what it's about,' I said.

'Machinery.'

'Yes! It's your machinery!' And I went over it all again. 'Day and night! Thump thump thump! I can't sleep! All day and all night!' I'd said it so often. No more I could say. I took a deep, deep breath and I let her have it. 'Is it you?'

Esther screamed like a fishwife, 'NO! IT IS NOT ME!'

In a moment she was apologising. 'Oh sorry, sorry.' And almost laughing. 'It's the broken night I expect.' As if mine hadn't been broken too. 'Sam said – I said – We agreed I'd go softly softly – I'd try to be patient –'

What has she got to be patient about? I'm the victim here!

December

It's no better. Thump, thump, thump. I phoned the landlady. I was in tears. 'I can't stand the noise. And if I speak to her about it she shouts at me.'

I heard the landlady sighing. 'I'll phone her and get back to you,' she said.

And she did. 'Esther says she's reading,' was her report. 'So is her son. They haven't even got the telly on and the cat's asleep.'

What cheek. 'Does that sound likely to you?' I yelled.

'Well, yes, it does,' the landlady said. 'There's never been any trouble with them before.'

'She's got a cat! Pets are not allowed!'

The landlady sighed again. 'She's an owner-occupier,' she said. 'There's nothing in the title deeds about pets. She can have all the pets she wants, unless they cause a nuisance. I don't think her cat does.'

I'm not so sure about that.

I tackled Esther about it. She looked startled. 'Busy road, our last cat was run over,' she said, 'we keep this one indoors.'

'She's committed a nuisance on the stairs.'

'She can't have. She doesn't get out.'

'What do you call this then?' I demanded, pointing to the landing.

Esther looked at me. 'I call it chewing-gum,' she said. 'The paper boy or the window cleaner,' and she stamped away.

There's far too much coming and going on this stair. I phoned the landlady. Didn't get much change out of her. 'Well, it's nearly Christmas,' she said.

'I know that, thank you very much,' I said. 'I'm having twenty people for Christmas dinner, if you want to know.'

I hear people coming in after midnight and some of them don't even live here. When I open my close door and peer out, there's no one there. But they are there. I can feel them. The cold stone, the fear. Just one bare bulb. The enemy in the sky. The old man from upstairs had his radio on. 'Dropping paratroopers,' he said. Somebody tried to shut him up. 'They'll be everywhere,' he said, 'you'll see.'

I need to know who's outside the door.

I found a firm in the yellow pages and got them to fix a CCTV camera above my close door. From my bedroom I can see who's going up and down the stairs. If they come, I'll see.

The landlady came round. Some man on the top floor is kicking up a fuss. 'The close is common property and he says CCTV is an invasion of residents' privacy,' she said.

I said 'Am I to be killed in my bed?' And they don't always kill you, not till you tell them what they want to know.

'I'll talk to him,' she said.

When she went away the noise came back. Thump, thump, thump. I went into the kitchen and knocked on the ceiling. That is, Esther's floor. I can do it by standing on a chair.

Knocking up hasn't helped. I phoned the landlady. I told her my suspicions. All of them. I went into every detail.

Finally she said 'All right. I'll phone Environmental Services. That should settle it for you.'

'For her, you mean,' I said and slammed the phone down.

Environmental Services came round after ten o'clock. They rang my bell! 'What are you doing here?' I screamed. 'The nuisance is upstairs!'

'Sorry to disturb you,' they said. 'We're obliged to speak to all parties. We can confirm there's no noise registered on our machine.'

'What about the laundry?' I yelled.

'No indication of laundry,' they said. 'Or other unusual activities.' They went away. No help at all.

I rang Esther's bell mid-morning. 'Get that machinery off!' I yelled. 'Me and the landlady, we're on to you, we're getting all the authorities on to you, you had an example of that last night!'

'Environmental Services found nothing,' she said in her cheeky way.

'How do I know that?' I screamed.

'Because they gave you a copy of their bloody report,' she said, and shut the door.

I heard a murmur of voices behind the panel. She opened the door again. 'Sam points out that you're going to report me to the landlady for swearing at you,' she said. 'Just to bring you up to date. I've written to her. A formal letter of complaint. With a copy to the property manager. It's the usual procedure in a case of harassment. Happy Christmas.' And she shut the door. For keeps this time, though I knocked and hammered and leaned on the bell.

January

The landlady asked how my Christmas dinner went. Nosy bitch. 'Their car broke down,' I said.

I had to go to Esther's door again. There's an unbearable vibration in my flat. The whole bed is shaking. 'I don't believe I have noticed that,' she coolly said. She called over her shoulder to her son: 'Sam, has your bed been vibrating?' He called something or other in reply with his mouth full, typically uncouth. 'Chance'd be a fine thing,' it sounded like to me.

As she shut the door I heard him say 'Has she dropped the laundry idea then?'

I hammered on the door and screamed, 'It's the laundry that's causing the vibration!'

'I thought it might be,' cheeky Esther said.

The close was full of the vibration. Shaking as if the house would come down. The planes going over. The noise in the sky.

I stopped her in the close. 'It's your printing machine, isn't it?' I said.

'Well, that makes a change,' she said.

'You're a writer,' I said. 'You're printing out your books.'

'The mighty presses roll, eh?' Esther said.

'Don't deny it. You're printing out your books. That's what it is. Day and night.'

'I have a small printer,' Esther said. 'It's about the size of a cornflakes box. If I ran it day and night it would probably burst into flames.'

I went away and called the police.

They came round about half-past eleven. Apparently Esther let them in to check the washing machines, though she's never allowed me into her flat. After that they came to me. Not the least bit helpful. The constable was all hung about with implements. What are they for? I'm sure there was somebody else out on the landing. In plain clothes. Sleek and cruel. They're the worst.

'Can you hear the machinery just now?' the constable said.

'Of course I can. I've told you again and again. Day and night.'

'Well,' he said, 'the lady upstairs has a domestic washing machine, which isn't on. And a small personal printer, which isn't on. Even if they were on, neither of them could possibly cause the kind of noise you're complaining about.'

'What is it then?' I screamed.

They had no answer. 'There's no noise,' said the sergeant, a sour-looking man, 'and that will go on the police computer.'

They went away. I kept an eye on the close through the CCTV in case they'd left a plain clothes man. There's an odd shadow by the back door.

I was up at Esther's door at 2 a.m. screaming 'Get that machinery off!' Unexpectedly it was her son who answered. I wouldn't like to tell you what he called me. I ran downstairs and he actually came after me. Esther was calling 'No, Sam,' and I heard him say 'We've tried everything else.' I just managed to get in and lock the door. I pushed the bolts across. Thank heaven it's an old door with strong bolts. They won't get in.

He hammered and knocked on my door. I stood there in the dark with this man's voice like a knife in my ears.

I think he called the police then. I remember standing in the icy cold close talking to them. Under one bare bulb. Their uniforms. The noise in the sky.

March

I think it's March. I've been very ill.

The landlady came round. It wasn't even rent day. 'Can I get in touch with somebody, Jenny?' she said. 'Family? Friends?' I told her to go away.

I'm all right now. It was the cold and the dark. One bare bulb and sometimes it blew. We huddled in the dark with the noise in the sky. When the door opened I saw uniforms there and screamed. The next-door baby was ill. Meningitis. I think it died.

I was ill too. My mother came to get me out of hospital. We stood and waited for a tram. Big empty spaces where the houses used to be. A cold wind blowing over the stones. Just a wall across the street and you could see where the four rooms had been. One above the other, a tenement, four floors. Wallpaper. Fireplaces still there.

'Did the Germans come?' I said.

'Not yet,' my mother said.

I'm strong enough now to start knocking on the ceiling again. I climbed up on the chair and I nearly fell off, but it works just the same if I knock on the wall.

'You'll have to stop doing that,' the landlady said.

I found Esther in the phone book. That was a good idea of mine. I phoned her about half past midnight. She sounded quite drowsy when she picked it up.

'You've got the TV on!' I accused her. 'Or the video! Switch it off now and never switch it on again!'

I heard her yawning. 'Gone mad again, have you, Betty?' she said sleepily.

'I'll report you for that!' I screamed.

'Oh, sorry, sorry,' she said. 'I would observe political correctness if I was awake. Goodbye.'

'It's you that's mentally disturbed!' I said, and rang off. Now she knows.

I've kept knocking, even though it doesn't do any good. I knocked after midnight and I yelled then too. Again about two o'clock. Again about four. In the morning I found Esther in the close talking to that bad-tempered man from the top floor. 'That is you, isn't it,' she said, 'the knocking? John can hear it three floors up.'

'What if it is?' I said.

'I thought at first it was somebody putting up shelves,' Esther said, 'but Sam pointed out they'd have to have more shelves than Ikea.'

'And you can tell him to stop playing that guitar too,' I said.

'Heard him recently, have you?' Esther said. I should have known she was going to be cheeky, that lazy voice of hers.

'Day and night!'

'Only he's moved into a place of his own,' Esther said. She said to the top-floor man, cutting me dead, 'He's been meaning to but he didn't want –'

'Yeah,' said the top-floor man.

Esther said, 'Everything went quiet so he thought it was safe to go. Six weeks ago. If he's playing his guitar day and night he's doing it in Maryhill.'

'Amazing how sound travels,' the top-floor man said.

April

No better. I looked out of the window to make sure it was clear. There was a man across the street.

I checked the close through the CCTV. Esther was on her way to the bins. She looked at my door as she passed. Furtively. She was carrying something she didn't want anyone to see.

I rushed out and caught her on the way back. She jumped. Guilty conscience. I could tell.

'Get that machinery off!' I screamed.

'Jenny –'

'Day and night!'

Sounds go strange in the close. My voice was going round and round, knocking against the walls. Like the baby crying. Like the noise.

'And that son of yours! He's helping you!'

'I've told you,' she said, 'he isn't here.' I had the feeling she couldn't think of anything else to say.

'He's been here!' I cried. 'I've seen him! Carrying things up and down the stairs!'

'He's moving his stuff out –'

She was trying to make some excuse but I didn't give her the chance. I kept screaming. And I don't mind saying I was swearing too. When I'd finished she just stood there. White as a sheet.

'Jenny –' she said.

'You are a sick woman!' I cried. 'Action will be taken! I'll see to that!' And I went indoors. I phoned the landlady and reported that I gave Esther hell.

What a lot of nonsense. The landlady has been here again. 'You're responsible for my health and happiness,' I reminded her. 'I still have my lease.'

She said, 'Next time I'll know what to include.'

According to her, police and social services are now involved. Not before time. They'll deal with Esther. It's high time somebody did. It took them long enough in the high flats too. Rowdy parties. Washing machines. A printing press.

A policeman came round to speak to me. The landlady hovered at the door. He told me there's nothing happening upstairs. I have to stop knocking up, he said. I have to stop harassing them.

'Me harassing them!' I said. 'I haven't had a wink of sleep for months!'

It looked as if they were going. Nothing settled! No proceedings! I said 'What happens next?'

He hummed and hawed. 'Probably not much,' he said.

'It's an illegal laundry!'

'Probably not a case for, er –' He looked everywhere but straight ahead. As if he was reading from a book he said, half to the landlady and half to me, 'There are a number of people in the community with problems which annoy neighbours but can't be addressed by social or psychiatric services.' And he shot out of the door as if he'd said too much.

Problems! She certainly has! I don't know why he's telling me!

I rang her doorbell at half-past midnight. 'Get that machinery off!' I yelled. She mentioned the police. I hurried downstairs. I was breathless when I got to the close. Had to stop before I went inside. Like the shelter. No air. Thump, thump, thump, in the sky.

I saw Esther in the close with a suitcase and hurried out to catch her. 'I'm off for a few days,' she said, 'I'm sure you'll be glad to know.'

'Getting fresh supplies,' I sneered.

'Well, no,' she said, 'talking to writers' groups. They tend to be slightly eccentric, so that will be a pleasant change.'

'Who's running the laundry then?'

'Gosh, I don't know,' Esther said. 'There's only the cat and she's strictly forbidden to use the washing machine.'

It hasn't made any difference. Thump, thump, thump.

And now men going up and downstairs. Heavy boots. I looked through the CCTV but they'd just turned the corner of the stairs. Jackboots echoing in the close.

I was knocking on the ceiling when I heard them again. I crept out and one of them was there. Leather jacket, fair hair cropped short, little round spectacles that reflected the light. So you don't know if they're looking at you. No smile. Though it's worse if they smile.

He saw me, though I tried to keep out of sight. 'Hi, Jenny,' he said.

They know my name! Maybe I screamed.

'Hey, hey,' he said. 'You know me. Sam? Esther's son?'

They'll say anything of course.

'I've just come back to feed the cat while Mum's away,' he said. 'I heard you knocking as I opened the door to go in. Really there's no need to knock when the flat's empty. The cat hardly ever operates heavy machinery.'

I think that's what he said. This is very bad.

I phoned the landlady. 'You've got to help me,' I said. 'The Gestapo are here.'

'The what?' she said. She's only young. She's never heard the name.

'They've tracked me down,' I said. 'You've got to find me another flat.' One that they don't know about. One where I'll be safe. And all the time the thump, thump, thump in the sky. I found the broomstick and knocked on the ceiling. It made no difference. They're lying in wait. 'I've got to go somewhere they can't find me,' I said.

'Well, Jenny,' she said, 'I don't think I'm going to make difficulties if you break your lease at this point. Where are you thinking of going?'

'You don't suppose I'd tell you, do you?' I said. It's all too clear now. She's in league with them.

May

I've been so cunning. I've found another place. The sun was streaming into the close when I viewed it and there was nobody about. It was bright, it was almost warm. Nothing like the shelter under the stairs.

I packed quickly and called a taxi. I'll post the keys back. No one knows. I suppose I should phone cousin Bella. She won't care.

The taxi passed a tenement that looked familiar and I realised why. It's where I lived two years ago, before the high flats. I had trouble there too. I certainly hope there's no trouble in the new place.

The South Side

She slid away and the flames roared high, or they did in his head. Dirty red flames, oil-stained, against the black city sky. One star pricked through the smoke and that was his sign.

See the star? One star up there? The blonde head lifted from his shoulder and that's when –

One, two, three.

No. No. No.

He put his mind on other flames. Like a gas cooker, would it be, little popping blue flames in two rows? You'd need more fire than that to eat through the wood, what was left of the flesh, the thin chicken bone. Flames all around. Like a car-wash. He choked on a sad sort of laugh.

The velvet curtains had whispered shut so that you couldn't see the flames, and behind the minister's trumpet-voice you couldn't hear anything at all. They stood up to sing *Abide With Me.* Margaret's family, melted in tears. He wasn't crying. Hadn't cried. That's all right, a man doesn't cry.

Behind him he heard sniffling, though that pew had been assigned to the neighbours and they didn't know Margaret well. High hedges, closed front doors, in the quiet and settled south side. But there was sniffling and sobbing. He angled his head above the hymn-book, and sure enough it was the woman next door, the sort of fool who'd cry for poorly kittens and road-kill. Her soft face, not young, was ugly with tears.

Beyond her he saw a blonde girl. A tall girl in black, her head bent for Margaret and for him. He saw the clean line of her cheek under the sweep of blonde hair.

What will I do now she isn't here?

He hung in empty space. Deep space. Shields down. Danger, great danger. What will I do?

And Margaret stood beside him, slipping her hand into his.

'You can't be here,' he said to her, though nobody could hear him under the last soaring notes of the hymn. Abide with me. She smiled and pressed closer. He felt the comfort of her body all down his side. He could count every thread in the sleeve of her old tweed coat. Her chapped hand with the wedding-ring was as solid as his own. 'You're looking after me, aren't you?' he said.

The undertaker was bowing before him, ushering him out of the pew. He made the polite gesture of letting Margaret go first, but of course she wasn't there. Heels clicked on the flooring behind him as he led the little procession down the aisle. High heels, a long-legged young stride. They came out of the crematorium chapel into the air and the blowing leaves, where other sad people thought about death.

'Matthew,' said the minister, wringing his hand as if they were old friends. 'It isn't finished, you know.'

'I know. I know.' High heels crunched on the gravel, going by.

'Death shall have no dominion. Gone but not forgotten. Anything I can do,' the black robes said.

'I'm not one of your parishioners.'

'As if that matters!' Rosy young face above the black and white, thinking it knew the score. 'And I knew Margaret so well.'

'She never missed a Sunday.' Though how much she had enjoyed it he couldn't say. He had sometimes met her after the service, walking the few hundred yards under the green south-side trees, past the heavy houses, each with its gates, its gravel drive and perfect lawn, its high hedge closing secrets in. Her face lit up when she saw him with a kind of relief. Her arm tucked into his, anchoring him to their safe life together again.

He was a crippled ship, drifting, now.

He looked across the courtyard and there she was among the grieving people, her anxious eyes fixed on him.

'Matthew?' the minister said.

'I sometimes think she's still here,' he said. 'More than think. Feel.'

'You'd be surprised,' the minister said, nodding briskly, 'just how common that feeling is. For a time. It passes.'

He maundered on, earnestly explaining, building a city on sand. 'Sometimes I think it's where we got the idea of a guardian angel.' Matthew looked over to where she had been. A comforting illusion. She had been there. She wasn't there now.

'Matthew, won't you come back with us? Just for a minute or two?'

It was the woman next door, red-eyed still. He didn't know, because Margaret wasn't there, whether that would be dangerous or not. She took his arm as his mother used to do. 'Just a few people. Long journey.' She was talking about Margaret's family, who were glooming at Matthew because he hadn't laid on funeral baked meats in a hotel. How could he, a man on his own?

A touch on his arm steered him into a car. An exchange of nods with the undertaker and the woman next door got in beside him. Settled him in, made sure he had shut the door properly. Like his mother. He gave her a clenched smile.

'Cup of tea, you'll feel better. Can't go home from a funeral to an empty house.' Fresh tears welled in her puffy eyes, though she was too old to cry.

I'll give you something to cry about.

No.

The woman didn't know, couldn't know, that her busy house with its teenagers and dogs was just as empty as his. Emptier, he thought as the next-door living-room fell open around him, bare as the surface of the moon: pine sofas, venetian blinds, waxed bare boards. Margaret had quilted their own floors with warm red carpets, fenced the mantelpiece with ornaments, draped the windows, wrapping him safe. He began to plan his life without her. He'd sit all day on her sofa, feet on her carpet, breathing her velvet-dusty air.

She used to sit like that in their soft safe living-room, skirt tucked over her knees, looking up from her needlework to check that all was well with him. She had made the velvet cushions that eased his tense spine, she had sewn the curtains that closed out the world with their heavy red folds. He wouldn't change anything, he'd keep the carpets and curtains cocooning him, and so he'd be safe, though Margaret was gone. Gone but left her soft furnishings. The treacherous panic giggle threatened again.

But the doorbell would ring and he'd have to answer it, because she wasn't there. Outside, behind the postman and the window-cleaner, the bare streets went north to a river running cold under a dark sky. Before you got to the river there were great stretches of the south side to go through.

The next-door daughter, long-legged and blonde, crossed the room towards him, bearing his cup of tea.

No. No.

'You won't have made any plans yet,' the woman next door was murmuring, and proceeded to answer herself, 'Of course not. It's too soon.'

'I don't – I can't seem to – I've nothing really to do.' Alone in the big house, huddled on Margaret's sofa, a red velvet cushion in his arms. Outside, a whole city, bleakly open, waiting for him. 'You know I took early retirement when she – when we – when it was diagnosed.' I haven't had to make plans, he thought, for thirty years.

But the neighbours knew him as a businessman, a decisive kind of guy. 'I think I'll have to move,' he said. 'I think it would be best. Memories.'

Emptiness roared around him, black flames hot on his threatened skin. The woman nodded as if she could understand. He wrenched himself away, if only in his mind; sat himself down in his living-room, safe at home, as the clock chimed ten and Margaret came in with supper on a tray. On his sofa, Margaret's sofa, the blonde daughter from next door crossed her long black legs.

No. No. Against the bleak lines of window-frame and floor she glowed, a dusky flame. She was in mourning but that couldn't save her: he stripped it all away and found the tender skin. The glimmer in her eye was like a single star. One, two, three.

No. No. What will I do?

He looked away from the tall blonde girl. Looked for Margaret, who would save him. Looked for her old tweed coat, but she had discarded it in the hall and there she came through the door, with her gentle smile, bundled hair, fluttering skirts, unchanged.

The hostess went forward to meet her. Could see her. That was a surprise.

Of course she wasn't Margaret, though as pretty and untidy. She was apologising for lateness, blaming the bloody traffic and her bloody car. Inoffensive feminine swearwords, Margaret's very trick of speech. She stopped in the doorway, looking for the widower, here to pay her respects. He had to be pretty obvious, hunched up in his blacks. At last, in his weariness, he was near to tears.

She crossed the room and took his weak hands in hers. 'Matthew, you don't know me,' she said. 'I'm Margaret's friend Louise. Can I fill your cup?'

1

Matthew stood at the clean gleaming window of his executive flat. That's what it had been called in the estate agent's shiny brochure. Maybe he wasn't exactly an executive these days, but Louise more than filled the bill. Which was okay. He supposed.

From here he looked down on the Merchant City, old but new, where smooth stone cliffs, inset with glass, preened golden in the low city sun, the thin sun of very early spring. Self-conscious skinny saplings instead of the fine trees of the suburban south side. No lawns or hedges, of course, at all. A weathercock glinted beyond the sheer warehouse walls, reflected in double-glazing, but out of kilter, not quite true.

How did I get here?

Since Margaret died, it seemed to him, he had been living in a muddled dream. He remembered trays of diamonds, after somebody said that Margaret's engagement ring really wouldn't do. Who said it? The woman next door? Louise? He remembered lawyers, estate agents, removal men; stiff documents and flimsy counterfoils; he remembered writing his signature again and again. The woman next door, all smiles. The minister, beaming, a goal scored for God. Everybody so pleased that he had found Louise.

Or that she had found him.

Doesn't matter. She's my guardian angel. She's Margaret, really. Nothing has changed.

The bland sun dazzled on the pane and now he saw the room behind him reflected in the window-glass, all washed in soft red. Margaret's curtains and carpet and sofa, cushions and china ornaments, transferred from the big south-side house to the new flat, just as he'd planned. They'd had to have the curtains and carpets drastically cut down for these new-style windows and economy-size rooms. 'Might be just as well to buy new,' Louise had frowned at the tape-measure.

'We can't afford it, dear,' he said out of long habit.

'I can,' she said in surprise, an executive lady of independent means.

But then she looked more closely at him and her foolish loving eyes moistened in sympathy with his. 'If it's really important to you – '

'It is.' He couldn't explain why.

Now, although this new room was so much smaller, he moved with sure knowledge among Margaret's chairs and chiffoniers, and even Louise wasn't bumping into them quite so much. 'Oh sugar!' she'd yell, clutching her hip-bone. 'I bruise easy, Matthew, you know!'

'So did Margaret.' At first he'd thought perhaps he shouldn't say that sort of thing, but she didn't seem to mind. 'Well, who's to see it but me?' he teased. He kissed it better, the soft skin with the quick blood just below. She liked that.

As Margaret had. He could still hardly believe, sometimes, how lucky he was. A new start, a new wife, but essentially, safely, exactly the same.

He stared out of the window. Not exactly the same. In the big house on the south side, where old trees spread their canopies of leaves, he had never needed to stand at the window wondering when Margaret would come home. The sun was down, leaving the old streets tired and grey.

Too much too soon. Drifting. Out of control.

A gull slipped on the spring wind past his window, but it was in control. It landed on the sill and stared him out with its cold eye. He saw the blood-scarlet spot on its yellow bill before it lifted and tilted off wide-winged, past the polished warehouses and the railway bridge, to the black river two streets away.

No. No. Danger there. Where are you, Louise?

He turned round into the familiar living-room. Margaret was sitting on the sofa, her sewing on her lap, patting the velvet cushions into place for him.

Tears flooded his eyes. When he blinked them away she had gone.

'Don't go,' he said. 'I need you.' But the lift hummed and its door hissed, and Louise's key turned in the lock.

She stood laughing in the doorway, peeling off layers of shawls, unzipping her long boots, throwing her briefcase on a chair. 'Oh God, what a day!' she cried. 'I had a fight with Gareth. Hand-to-hand combat. Gareth! What a name!'

'That's why you didn't come home for lunch.'

She flicked him a look, doing something with her hair. 'Well, it was never very likely, love.' But she came across for her kiss. It was a long one, he couldn't stop; he hadn't had her for eight hours or more.

Her apple-blossom scent filled his nose and he was back in Louise's bedsit, the stuffy room reached by the long stone stair. Sweet scent and virginal clumsiness, though indeed, after Margaret's long illness, Matthew hadn't been what you'd call adept himself. After the clumsiness, a vast and easeful relief. That he remembered very well.

An oddness teasing the edge of his mind, something he'd noticed even in the glowing blissful moment, wouldn't quite come clear.

'Hey, ow,' she complained, laughing in his grip. Maybe she'd bruise. Another few hours, when the clock chimed bedtime and she gave her signal yawn, and then she'd see. No, he'd see. He shook his head impatiently to straighten out his thoughts.

She'd had enough and slipped out of his slackened arms. 'Got the kettle on?' She didn't wait for an answer, since she knew what it would be. 'I swear I don't know what you do all day.' But it didn't really worry her and she went whistling into the kitchenette.

'When you're not here to look after me,' he said. She wouldn't hear, he knew, as the water ran and the crockery clinked. He kept his voice light and merry, all the same.

She popped her head out, frowning a bit. Younger than Margaret, sharper ears, remember that. No, she was only checking the room: 'You might clear a space for the tray, love.' Plenty of little tables, but Margaret had been fond of fruit-bowls, vases, china shepherdesses and puppy-dogs, and there they all were in the cosy living-room, where they belonged. He removed the *Herald*, two videos and a stack of detective stories from the coffee-table beside his chair and Louise brought in the tray. Matthew sat back and felt his very bones relax. He hadn't relaxed during all the long day alone.

Louise sat opposite, smoothing her long skirt over her knees, pouring tea, passing biscuits, as Margaret used to do. 'Nothing home-baked! Guaranteed!' she carolled. A difference there. He had a glimpse of Margaret's flushed face and felt the heat from the busy oven. She had scorned the very idea of a microwave. The kitchen here came fully fitted, double oven, grill and rotisserie, but the micro and the dishwasher seemed to be all Louise ever used.

But Louise is here. Remember that too. Margaret isn't. Is she? He slid a glance sideways and saw the warm terracotta weave of her tweed skirt. He held out his cup for her to refill, but it was Louise's plump hand adjusting the tea-cosy, tilting the pot.

She took another chocolate biscuit for herself, leaving him to stretch for his. 'Now I've got something to tell you,' she said through the crumbs. 'Two things.'

'Nice things?' he said, on edge at once again. Though why?

She raised casual brows. 'Well, I think they're nice, you may not,' she said. 'The second one's nice. Libby, you know, Gareth's PA, she's down with flu, that's not very nice, right enough.' Never one word when five would do. Such a blether, same as Margaret. A comfortable way to be.

'The office is all upside-down. They wanted archive stuff for the new promotion and I had to go to the Mitchell. Right across town! Can you imagine? Old newspapers! It's not my sort of thing.'

Her warm voice maundered on, wrapping him round like a comfort blanket. He ate another biscuit, thinking about bed.

'Dixon's Blazes,' she said.

He blinked. Smoke and flames.

She was looking at him oddly. 'What's that again?' he had to say.

'I said do you remember them? Old ironworks? Glasgow icon, yeah? South side?'

'Not really,' he said. 'It wasn't my bit of the south side.'

'I'd never bloody *heard* of them. Pulled down long ago. I had to go back to nineteen-fifty-*nine* or some damn year.'

'Bound volumes in a basement.' Why did he remember that?

'Well, no, not now. You get the lift to level five and it's all on microfilm. Cute little boxes. Only I kept getting it inside-out.' She proceeded to describe her travails in the library with such a wealth of humorous detail that he stopped listening altogether.

But again he'd missed something he should have heard. She had stopped blethering; she was looking at him, awaiting his reply. A bit uncertain? This must be the not-nice thing.

'Sorry? What say?'

She clicked her tongue. 'I have to go back to work tonight. *Client* meeting. Standing in for *Libby*.'

'When?' he heard himself whine.

'Well, now, really. I'll leave you a salad.'

'Oh God, Louise.' Matthew scrutinised her for signs of remorse. She ducked her head, but only, as it proved, to focus on a few biscuit crumbs, dabbing them up into her mouth with a licked finger, like a large child. 'You could have said you were needed at home,' he reasonably pointed out. 'Margaret always used to.'

Shouldn't have said that perhaps.

'No, I couldn't, Matthew!' Hardly a laughing matter, but she was giggling away. 'Sorry, my husband can't make his own supper!' She saw his face. 'Oh hey! Don't I do enough for you then?' And she slipped on to the sofa beside him.

Annoyed as he was, his hand cupped her soft breast. He couldn't help it. Into his ear she breathed: 'You could always go out for a pizza.' She was serious about that. She really didn't seem to know what she was doing to him.

'I might.'

Margaret's worried brown eyes in the mahogany and crimson hall: 'You're not going out, Matthew? By yourself?' And he would take her upstairs instead.

Usually. Nearly always. In a sick panic he wrapped his arms round Louise.

But she pushed herself away from him. She sat up straight, hardly ruffled, draining her cup of tea with a childish gurgling noise. 'What's the nice thing then?' he enquired through gritted teeth.

'Oh, it's the office party. Only it's tomorrow, not next Friday, I got the date wrong. And I shouldn't have, very naughty smack bottom. First of March, it's only the firm's tenth bloody birthday, that's all.' Glancing up as she collected the teacups, she pulled a face to match his. 'A bit much for you, poor old Matthew. All this socialising, eh?'

She slipped on to the sofa again and this time she sank on to his knee, winding her arms round his neck. 'No, this is different. Spouses, partners, significant others invited. And you're my spouse. Least I think you are.'

She was wriggling. She did know what she was doing. 'I think so too,' he said. 'First of March? That's our three-months anniversary.'

She hadn't had time to shower yet and he got a whiff of secret warmth. She always insisted on showering first, but God, not now surely. She must know. He pulled her deeper into his lap. I want it now. Right here. Had he said that aloud?

But they might as well have been back in her bedsit. There it was, the awkwardness, the reluctance, though three months of married life should have cleared all that away. 'Come on,' he said, 'you started it.' The oddness nearly took shape and form, but he had more to think about, fumbling in the flowing woolly skirts.

'Oh sugar, is that the time?' She jumped up and whisked the tray into the kitchenette.

I could have kept her. I can make her stay.

No. No.

'You'd better come to the party,' her voice floated back. 'Else you'll have to make your own supper again.' She emerged with the kettle in her hand, Margaret's kettle, once shiny and new. 'This thing is making funny noises. I think it's reached the end of its useful life. Look, couldn't you run down to Argos tonight? They're open late.'

He couldn't believe what was happening. She knew what he wanted but she didn't care. 'You could look for the same model,' she was coaxing, coming across and kissing the top of his head. 'You'd like the same one, wouldn't you?'

'I might. Something to do while you're out,' he said, as one hand gripped the other convulsively in his lap.

2

He didn't go to Argos, though.

Louise, all lipstick and eyeshadow, had just whirled out to her client meeting when a capful of cold rain blattered on the windowpane. It wouldn't last, spring showers, and he dithered over waiting or making a run for it.

'No hurry! Tomorrow will do!' he heard Margaret say. 'Look, I'll turn out the kitchen cupboards today and then I can come with you tomorrow.' He couldn't quite hear Louise saying the same. Turning out cupboards wasn't her wet-weather pastime of choice. In fact she never put anything back in the kitchen cupboards. Coffee-mugs, sugar, biscuits, all sat out on the worktop as if she was still in her bachelor-girl bedsit.

Where she'd had a kettle just like Margaret's. He saw it quite clearly, same vintage, same unfashionable blocky chrome, on the ricketty table by the gas stove. Louise didn't seem to recall her bedsit, treasure its memory, as vividly as he had reason to do. She had bundled everything up, no selection, no discarding, and the kettle would be in the boxes now.

He opened the door of the little back room, full of tea-chests and cartons, hardly a square yard of floor-space free. Into this small Merchant City flat, really meant for a first-time buyer, they had crammed everything from the big south-side house and from the bedsit too. The removal men had prophesied doom as box after box came in, and they'd had to dump a lot of it in the back room, which was going to be a second bedroom or maybe a study some day. Before long he had got the south-side stuff deployed in the living-room, creating the home he had planned, his and Margaret's belongings in place as they used to be. Louise's stuff still wasn't fully unpacked. Nowhere to put it, was there?

In the living-room it wasn't hard to hold on to Margaret. She was everywhere there, delicately inhabiting her burgundy curtains and china dogs, her fragile teacups and well-stuffed easy chairs. In the boxes there was no one but Louise.

He opened the first box and the smell of Louise came out in a puff of stale air. Her shampoo? Her talc? After showering, before sex, she powdered every crevice. He felt the cool slippery powder under his fingers, between his skin and hers.

It was the smell of her bedsit too. He had escorted her home after their first date, just as he'd always escorted Margaret. ('Date?' Louise said as if he was talking a foreign language, but she saw he was embarrassed and let it go.) He hadn't a clue where to take her, but amazingly he remembered the name of the restaurant where he had courted Margaret, and phoned to book a table for two.

It was a new place trading under the old name. Not the same. Louise ate one-handed in the American way and they didn't find much to talk about. Between the steak and the trifle he had a flash of insight: that sometimes happened with him. She's waiting for something, he thought.

True enough, as he found.

He rummaged through the first box but found no kettle, just some paperbacks, a bathmat, a small folding Christmas tree and three pairs of shoes. Not what you'd call methodical, our Louise. Two frying-pans, no wonder she was plump, and a heavy little stack of CDs. Did she have a CD player? He'd never seen it. They watched TV in the evenings till the clock chimed time for bed. To find space for a CD player in the living-room they would have to clear some of the ornaments away.

She got a bit testy dusting Margaret's ornaments, when she did dust, which wasn't frequently. No ornaments on her bedsit mantelpiece, as far as he could recall. A temporary sort of place. How long had she lived there? He hadn't asked her and even now he didn't really know. She hadn't seemed acquainted with anybody they met on the stairs. Young men and girls clattered past giggling, laughing at Matthew's hat, he gloomily supposed. Or his overcoat. Just as well they couldn't see the three-piece suit below.

No, it was the whole picture that he made with Louise: a man of his age and a woman of hers. Twenty years between them. Far too much, in the eyes of these young bucks and belles.

Far too much in his heavy heart, standing on Louise's doorstep, absolutely unsure about what she expected from him now.

The second box looked promising, with casseroles and a milk-jug, but still no kettle. A few more books, a couple of detective stories he'd never read. Not many books at all. Why did he think that was strange? Louise's bedsit bookshelves, in his memory, were as bleak and bare as the rest of the room. A box of Tampax, a flimsy nightie he'd never seen. He pushed its softness aside and found Louise's coffee-café-kaffee mugs. These he remembered very well indeed. She offered him a cup of coffee, and that's when it began.

Come on! Find the kettle!

He could see it beside the sink with the coffee-mugs and a carton of long-life milk. She was so awkward, so shy. The coffee-mugs, sadly wannabe bohemian, were printed with coffee-café-kaffee all over their heavy glaze. He studied each word while they sat on separate chairs making the most stilted conversation. What had he done with his life so far? Well, he'd lived with his mother until she died, and then he married Margaret. And what about you, Louise? Absolutely no life events to report, it appeared.

Matthew had to ask the way to the toilet and even that embarrassed her, she was so unused to men. A few tentative moves, when he came back, got nowhere at all. On his first date with Margaret he hadn't even tried, but he didn't know what girls expected nowadays. Looking at Louise as she perched on a straight-backed chair, he rather thought that she didn't know either.

He got up to go and they said goodnight in the hall. She had a full-length mirror there. He couldn't believe she ever looked in it, sparrow-dowdy as she was then. It coldly reflected his hands on her shoulders, his politely bowed head, ready to offer her a chaste kiss on the cheek. Goodnight and, he supposed, goodbye.

Until she latched on to him. Even now, in memory, it was a shock. She prised his mouth open, she kissed him with a desperate force. Only for a moment, but it was enough. He pushed her, or she pulled him, back into the room. It couldn't be stopped then.

He did have a good visual memory and he was back now in the dull neutral bedsit between the sink and the leatherette armchair. Louise backed towards the virginal narrow divan, her wide eyes fixed on something she'd clearly never seen before. Margaret was wont to close her eyes or delicately look away, so even she hadn't often seen it out and proud. Louise hadn't the faintest idea what to do.

Where the hell's that kettle?

The third box contained pillows and towels and the duvet from the bedsit divan, tired and faintly unclean, as the rest of the room had been. No use, of course, on the big double bed from the south-side house. Louise had laughed a bit at Margaret's blankets and eiderdowns, until he made it clear how hurtful that was to him. But his neighbours gave them a double duvet as a wedding present. 'Isn't this better, love?' coaxed Louise.

The next box was tied with string. As the knots came undone there was a different smell.

Skirts and jerseys, a tweed coat, a quilted dressing-gown, felt hats. Margaret's clothes.

He was swamped by loss, all direction gone. He buried his face in the rough wool, breathing comfort and safety and camphor mothballs. Margaret's smell.

What will I do now she isn't here?

He wrenched his mind away from that and applied it to practical things. How did this stuff get here? Well, the woman next door, of course. He hadn't dared even to look in Margaret's wardrobe himself, and the neighbours had breezed in, mum, dad and daughter, to help him pack. They must have thought he wanted to keep her clothes. Or didn't like to ask.

Or the blonde young daughter had packed them without a thought, never imagining what they meant. He saw her slim hands sorting and folding, holding a shabby coat up at the full stretch of her thin young arms. She bent over the box, all soft angles and long legs. She was lost in smoke and black flame. One, two, three.

No. No. What will I do?

He raised his head and saw Margaret standing by the door.

She couldn't be, because there wasn't room for her to stand among the piled-up boxes. She was definitely there. Thin sunlight from the window caught the lenses of her glasses, making her eyes look blank and blind. But she saw him. Saw him clearly. Loved him all the same. 'You're looking after me, aren't you?' he begged.

She only smiled. He knew she was saying yes.

'I need you, Margaret.' But she was gone.

Seeing her had settled him, as it always did. He tied up the box of clothes and ripped the tape off the next. Another great muddle of shoes, bath essence, knives and forks. And a bundle of letters held by a fragile rubber band.

Margaret's writing. His heart banged hard and sore.

They were all addressed to Louise. A long stretch of years in the postmarks, and a slew of different addresses, Manchester, Brighton, Aberdeen. Always Louise.

Louise had worked away from home a lot, which was why he'd never seen her before the funeral. (Or if he'd seen her, he hadn't noticed her. He didn't need to, with Margaret there.) He vaguely knew she'd moved from job to job. Young, unattached, no reason to settle down. She'd have moved on again soon, no doubt, found another job in another city, another Gareth and Libby, client meetings about something completely different. Except for that bizarre moment, two drifting ships colliding, in the bleak hall outside her bedsit room.

Only natural Margaret should write to Louise, her best friend. I ought to read them, Matthew thought, in case -

In case what? He shook his head.

He pushed the letters back into the box and purposefully rummaged again. With success: he pulled out Louise's kettle, the kettle from the bedsit; not new, not like the rest of her sleek kitchenware, but in pretty good order, flex smooth, plug firmly screwed together. Pleased with himself, stowing everything back in the box, he stopped at the letters again.

No, no, they're Louise's, can't go reading them. He slipped one cornerways out of its envelope. Chat and blethering: he heard Margaret's voice. Nice spell of weather. We've pruned the roses. A colour television at last - 'We sit at home a lot!!!' with lots of lively exclamation marks. Nothing there. What would there be?

But he was back in the south-side house, sitting on the sofa with Margaret beside him in her soft-washed old jersey and skirt. Apple-blossom scent hung round her, as round Louise. It was the same scent, he was sure.

How could it be?

On the sofa with Margaret. On the same sofa with Louise. It isn't going to work, he thought, and didn't know why.

But it's got to work. He levered himself to his feet and went back into the living-room, taking the kettle with him, leaving the letters behind.

They came with him, though. The sofa, Margaret's sofa, where she'd probably sat with her writing-pad on her knee. She would have talked to Louise through the letters, having no close friend at hand. You didn't make friends across the high hedges of the south side, over the rolling lawns. 'Who can I talk to?' he asked the china dogs. Should be able to talk to Louise. Used to tell Margaret everything. Not quite. No.

He sat on the sofa with tears streaming down his face. This happens, the doctor had said, the minister too. You think you're perfectly all right and then –

'I'll give you something to cry about,' said his mother, long ago.

'Margaret?' he said out loud in the dark-red room, designed to keep him safe. 'I need you, Margaret.'

But she wasn't there. He had the mad idea that she was sitting on her sofa, in her living-room, in the big house over on the south side.

I mustn't go to the south side.

Louise hadn't closed the curtains and the clear city evening came in. A lovely evening. Beside the weathercock blinked a single star.

Louise did say to go out.

It's a pilgrimage, if you like.

He went out and got a bus going to the south side.

3

And he stood on the lawn, under the full-leaved spreading trees. The hedges had grown high since they moved in, but he liked that and Margaret didn't seem to mind. He couldn't see the neighbours. Voices drifted on the summer air. One of them might be the blonde daughter's, but it was too faint to bring her into his mind. He was safe, cradled and comforted, on the gracious south side.

'Dinner's ready, Matthew,' said Margaret, smiling from the door. He blinked at her. The sun dazzled his eyes.

How could that be, in a February night?

The bus jolted over a pothole that shook the teeth in his head. He peered out of the dirty window and didn't understand. He had taken a bus to the south side, but this wasn't right. It wasn't his bit of the south side.

They had certainly crossed the river and they'd been juddering on for a long time. There ought to be trees and grass by now. Instead he saw a little bleak street, sharp-edged new flats, a bright off-licence with teenagers lounging outside. He wasn't used to buses. He didn't drive, never had; Margaret was only too happy to chauffeur him to and from work. In his new Merchant City lifestyle, buses didn't feature. He walked a few yards to the paper-seller's stall, or Louise jovially loaded him into her little car. He had only known what bus to take tonight because he remembered the street grid in the city centre, east-west, north-south, impossible to go wrong.

He had escaped like that before.

No.

With no idea what stop he wanted, he had asked for the terminus and couldn't believe how much he had to pay. He jammed two pound coins into the mean little slot, only to find that you didn't get change. The whole thing was a disaster. Bad idea from the start. He got up and moved forward to the door.

'This isny the terminus, Jim.'

Jim or John, he remembered from long ago. What they call you in Glasgow if they don't know your name.

'Near enough. That's okay.' As the bus crashed its gears and drove off he could almost hear the driver in conference with the old wifies going home from bingo. That's toffs for yez, eh! Money to burn, by the way! Disny know he's alive!

Matthew stood in the long dark street and wondered if he was.

He had found the south side, but not what he wanted, his and Margaret's south side. He was in another south side, where he hadn't been for thirty years. I was only looking for Margaret. It's Margaret's fault that I'm here now. He felt an anger rise that he hadn't ever felt for Margaret before.

Not quite true. No. No.

He dashed across the road, causing a car's brakes to scream and its driver to yell abuse. There was a bus stop opposite. It's all right. Nothing has happened and nothing will. I'll get a bus and soon I'll be back safe with Louise.

If there's a bus, that's to say.

As well as not knowing the fares, he didn't know the timetables. People walking past seemed to look at him curiously, as if no sane person would expect a bus at this time of night. Matthew fidgeted in the bus shelter. Taxis passed, slowing in hope of a fare.

Not a taxi. No.

In the shelter there was a rudimentary street map, meant for tourists. Something else that had changed: he couldn't remember ever seeing tourists in the city he used to know. Peering at the map, he saw the Merchant City, and the corner where, with relief, he had identified a southbound bus. Below that, though the grid system of streets basically held fast, two main routes slanted southwards. The left-hand road on the map, the western one, slipped smoothly across the river and soon it was veering to the south-west, through broad acres of restored red-sandstone tenements, beside a park, turning due south again towards quiet leafy streets. On the rough map he saw the very street where he and Margaret had been safe.

Tonight, disoriented as he was, he'd got a southbound bus all right, but one which followed the angular road shooting off to the south-east. That's where he had gone wrong.

Quite wrong. He'd never been here with Margaret. When they went into town they took the new bridge, swooping high and passionless above the swarming streets. No hope of finding it tonight, and anyway he thought it was only for cars. He began to walk.

He remembered high black tenements on either side, but what he seemed to be walking through were little breeze-block industrial estates. Buses came up from behind and passed him. Matthew let them go by.

The grid system carried on across the river and he shouldn't get lost here. But across the rectangles slashed the two main roads, splayed like legs, with a triangle of space between. On the sketchy tourist map the triangle between had been blank, but he thought there ought to be something there. He remembered factory chimneys, dirty smoke, leaping flame. What he saw were hard-faced flats with security lights, set back from the road, fronted by ribbons of concrete and bitten slabs of turf.

Stories about these flats were everywhere at one time. A recent time, so it was perfectly safe to replay them, sick or blackly funny as they were. The wifie with the wee dog. Interlinked piazzas designed for summer strolling. You'd take your life in your hands! Drug dealers gathered and dodged away. A different world. Another south side. No danger there.

He had never been in these mean streets before. His feet hurt and he began to feel like a fool. Definitely no chimneys, no smoke or flame.

He paused at another bus stop. No buses to be seen of course. He looked around for a cruising taxi. No harm now in getting a taxi, it's all gone. In the glare of the halogen lights you couldn't see a single star.

Ahead of him, as the road made a dog-leg, he saw the hunched half-turned shoulder of the dance-hall. Another step or two and the wide doorway came into view, welcoming dancers in on a Saturday night.

No.

But it was exactly the same. Squared-off art deco, gleaming white stucco. Above the door, painted in flat innocent colours, there spread like a peacock's tail the glittering belt of the zodiac, the stars and the moon. That was its name: The Moon and Stars. Silly name, he'd often thought. On a night of full moon you couldn't see the stars. When you saw a star, a single star, there wasn't a moon.

One, two, three.

He blinked. The brilliant halogen lights dimmed the real stars and the painted zodiac too. No, the zodiac was gone. Neon tubing scribbled a different name across the flat white frontage and the place was a disco, a club, something like that, now.

Not a dance-hall. No.

It was the same, though.

He stood among the same tenements, half a street left over from the bad old days. They had probably been upgraded like most of the city's tenements, double-glazed, stone-cleaned, but in the flashing disco lights you couldn't tell. Between flashes they were black and silent as they used to be, and the distant closes at the far end of the block held their blackness all the time. A girl came out of the blackness, hurrying past the closemouths to get into the light.

When she got there she wasn't pleased. Matthew had a good view from his bus stop across the street, and he surmised that she was late but the boyfriend was later. She stood under the flashing canopy of the disco, tapping her foot and swivelling to stare up and down the road. She asked a passing couple for the time. She pulled off her floppy velvet hat and ran a hand through her hair. It shone in the flashes, white and gold.

A hat? Is that a new fashion? They never wore hats then.

She crammed on the hat again, crushing the blonde hair, springy lively hair that would flatten and bounce up again like golden wire. She twisted again on her sharp high heels. Perhaps the boy had been there on time. He had given up and gone away. She would give up now. She would walk off into the darkness past the black closemouths where no light could reach.

Matthew bit the heel of his hand.

He fixed his mind on the new high flats. The programme he had watched, Margaret yawning at his side. The wifie, always a wee wifie at hand, telling the story about the dog. See thae high walkways? See on a windy day? See ma wee dug? Blown right aff its wee feet so it wis. Straight oot on the end o its lead like a balloon.

Matthew laughed out loud, and he shouldn't have. Another wee wifie, the very twin of the dog-owner, had joined him in the bus shelter. Always a wee wifie, sharp eyes, quick tongue.

But she laughed too, a dry croaky smoker's laugh, nodding at the bit of street theatre being played out across the road. She'd been watching the blonde girl with interest and she assumed Matthew had too, because at a Glasgow bus stop you had plenty of time to watch the passing show. The boyfriend had turned up at last. 'Christ, he's for it noo,' the wee wifie chuckled, knowing it all.

I'll give you something to cry about, said a hoarse voice in Matthew's head.

No.

The boy was trying to explain but the girl wasn't taking excuses. Shrill argument, fuck-laden, echoed across the road, causing the wifie to tut.

'Nae necessity for that,' she primly observed.

Why does she mind? She knows.

He could see the thin wedding-band sunk in the wifie's fat finger-joint. She's been there. The thought ran on and he couldn't stop it. It shook and worried him. An old wifie. He bit his hand again.

The boyfriend gestured hopefully towards the disco, but forget it! Fuck off! The girl stamped off down the street.

The boy stared for a moment. You could see a slow fuse start to burn. He ran after her and caught her by the arm. She wrenched her sleeve away, the short leather jacket half off her back.

'This yours, son?'

Matthew, shaking, turned.

The wifie was sticking her hand out to stop a lurching bus. Or a taxi. He couldn't make out the number, if it was a bus.

'Yeah, it'll do,' he said. The doors wheezed open and he got on after the wifie, jamming the maximum fare into the slot again. Praying she wouldn't notice when he got off far too soon.

No problem; she paid him no attention at all. She was craning her neck to catch a last sight of the boy and girl, both yelling now in the empty street. She had sat down next to another wifie and started to relate the whole story to her. Glasgow wifies: sharp eyes, quick tongues. Some things hadn't changed. Matthew drew his cuff down to cover the half-circle of toothmarks on his hand.

No problem either getting off the bus, since the wifie was still gabbing away. From the corner of the square he did see a potential problem, though. Five floors up, the living-room light was on.

'Louise,' he said. 'Didn't think you'd be in.'

'Well, I didn't think you'd be out.' A little frown between her thick eyebrows as she came over for her kiss.

Her head got in the way between him and the mantelpiece clock. He couldn't see the time and he needed to know. He wanted to throw her aside.

He collected himself and pulled her close instead. Surprised at first, she beamed and wound her arms round under his jacket, returning the favour with zeal. Through her ruffled hair he saw the hands of the clock. 'Half-past eight,' he observed.

'Did you think it would be later?'

'Not really. I wasn't sure. You did say I should go out.'

'Oh yes! So I did! Get something to eat, did you?'

He'd forgotten all about that. 'Just a pizza.'

'Oh, my lamb! And the awful thing is, the bloody meeting didn't take as long as we thought. I could have made supper when I got back.' She drew him on to the sofa, offering apologies and coffee. 'I'll put the kettle on. Oh no, blast, it's broken. You didn't get to Argos, I suppose?'

'Didn't need to. I found one in the boxes.'

'The boxes?'

'In the back room.'

'Oh yeah.'

'Your old kettle. From your bedsit.' He ran his hand up her leg from ankle to knee.

'Hey!' Perhaps she remembered the bedsit after all.

He felt her tremble, and, a breakthrough in its way; she didn't check the clock to see if it was officially bedtime. 'The fresh air's done you good,' was all she observed. A star in each bright eye, her breath dark flames. It's going to be all right, he thought. First time he had been nearly sure. He drew his finger down her rosy cheek, touched her parted lips. He cupped his other hand under a round breast where the nipple stood proud.

'I'll just have a quick shower.' Before he could grab her she was up and away.

She'd locked the fucking bathroom door. He sat on Margaret's sofa, gripping Margaret's velvet cushions in his arms. 'I was never angry with Margaret,' he said aloud in the red and mahogany room.

No. No.

I will never be angry with Louise.

He heard the shower stop; apple-blossom scent drifted through. He got up and crossed to the drinks trolley. She seemed perfectly delighted to be handed a glass of wine as soon as she opened the door, sweet and clean.

Matthew remembered warm young flesh, sweaty from dancing.

No.

By the time they had steered each other into the bedroom he had actually gone off the idea, but Louise was in her element. She sat neatly on the edge of their king-size bed, toed her slippers off, swung her legs up and in, and there she was, dimpling over the duvet, all prepared. She reached a round white arm to the bedside table for another sip of wine. She wore a big loose cotton t-shirt, practical enough, she had modestly explained, for he could reach both up and down.

Margaret lay primly beside him, winceyette buttoned to her chin. Like her, Louise always kept her nightie on. The lacy thing in the boxes, what about that? Matthew switched the light off, another preference Margaret had. No, Louise.

His nose tickled from the talcum powder. She'd even washed her hair. Her cottony marshmallow breasts brushed his cheek 'You don't have to keep your nightie on, you know,' Matthew said, raising his head.

Here in the cosmopolitan Merchant City it was never completely dark. A street-light shone through the curtains and caught a brightness in her eyes. 'I keep it on so you can take it off,' she breathed.

Two glasses of wine, for God's sake. Had she nipped at a few more between bedroom and shower? 'Is that what you want me to do?'

Louise stretched beneath him, arms flung up, bracing her toes against the foot of the bed. Certainly teasing now. 'Whether I want you to or not,' she said.

No. No.

He stripped the nightshirt off with workmanlike dispatch. She crooned and giggled; he could smell her toothpaste and deodorant, the dab of scent on her throat, sweet as a box of violet chocolate creams. Who told her this was the way to be? He plunged away and Margaret's letters came into his mind, folded into their faded envelopes, held tight with rubber bands.

'Did you enjoy that?' he courteously enquired, as he always had.

'Oh yes, it was lovely,' Margaret said. No, Louise.

'Good.' Situation normal. They turned back to back and settled down to sleep.

Margaret's letters got into his dreams. The first one he opened was a bus timetable. The second appeared to be a recipe for fudge, but he knew, in his dream, there was another meaning that he had to find. He scrabbled through the stack of envelopes, hundreds of envelopes, terror growing. He found he was hard again. That wasn't a dream.

He turned over in bed and felt Louise stir, restless, in reply. 'You awake?'

'Can't seem to get to sleep.' She reached for a scented tissue and blew her nose. 'We went to bed earlier than usual,' she said. 'That'll be it.'

They lay side by side like effigies on a tomb.

If she moved her hand just an inch or two, she'd feel – she'd know –

Why don't I just –

No. No. Blonde hair, long legs flickered in his mind. No.

89

'Clearing the boxes,' he said into the half-dark, 'you know? I found a lot of letters. From Margaret to you. You probably forgot they're there.'

She was absolutely still.

'Didn't read them, of course.'

She turned to him and wrapped him in her arms. He had rubbed off some of the sugar first time round and her own warm scent came through. 'A shock for you,' she murmured, 'finding them,' but that wasn't what her body said.

'I didn't read them,' he said once more. He touched her and she whimpered in joy.

He felt her mouth on him, butterfly kisses at first. 'This is what Margaret used to do,' she breathed. 'Isn't it?'

Margaret had never, never done that. Amazing, wild.

Blonde hair blew across his face. He rolled them both over, across the bed, anywhere, and the act drowned his questions and thoughts. This time they really fell asleep.

4

Next morning Louise was up with the lark. As she didn't fail to remark herself. She chirruped around the flat, bringing Matthew coffee and toast in bed. 'Lovely morning!' she cried with determined cheer from the living-room next door. 'Spring at last!'

Matthew heard her open the window, but, so early, the street sounds hardly came in. He thought he heard a brushing, a swishing of water, as somone swept and hosed away the grubbiness of the night, leaving the Merchant City clean as a child's box of bricks.

Maybe he was imagining that. He got up and looked out of the window, and of course no street-sweeper was to be seen, but the boxy buildings glittered in the early sun. Safe in their newness, just unwrapped. Uncontaminated. He had a quick flash of the south side, the old streets and old crimes. He'd never go there again.

He drank in the chiselled stone, the polished windows, where an old life had been made new. 'Yes, you know, I like it here,' he said to Louise as she whirled by. 'You look out and you see – There's nothing to see.'

'Bo-ring,' she carolled from the next room. 'What about the history, eh? Footpads? Screams in the night?'

The crying of the gulls, scavenging up from the black river, was the only disturbing noise.

He heard Louise yelp and slam the window shut. A moment later she appeared in the bedroom doorway, rosy with giggles yet slightly startled too. 'Footpads or what? Bloody seagull tried to get my toast!'

'That's the way the yuppies go on. They're always complaining about the gulls. Might have to be poisoned.'

'Poisoned? The yuppies?' she said in apparent alarm.

'No! The gulls!' Surely she wasn't laughing at him?

'Naah. Wouldn't work. See, they'd fall out of the sky on to people's heads.' She was off again, running from room to room, picking up jacket, bag, car keys where they lay. Her voice came echoing back from the different acoustics of the bathroom as she slapped on lipstick and twirled a mascara brush. Then she was whisking into the back room. The sound of feet on bare boards. What on earth did she want in there? As if in answer she bobbed up in the doorway again, tying a big silk scarf round her neck. He remembered seeing it in the boxes, and evidently Louise had remembered it too.

She came across and leaned over the bed for a quick goodbye kiss. That's what she intended; he held her and it went on and on. Her shirt was fresh from the iron, her jacket and skirt had a faint, tangy, dry-cleaning smell. If I took them off her? Into the office still trying to get her breath, creases across the pin-stripes, great thumb-holes in the top of her tights, though nobody would know but herself?

She giggled again as his hands went to and fro, but braced her feet on the floor and pulled away with unexpected strength. 'Behave! I'll be late! Gareth will go mad!'

Matthew didn't hear the flat door slam. When he saw the bedside clock clearly again, he couldn't believe the time. An hour at least had gone. The day stretched ahead, a wilderness of danger. He couldn't imagine what it might bring.

'I will never be angry with Louise', he said into the cold air.

He sat for a while on Margaret's sofa, channel-hopping, but of course there was nothing to engage his mind. Schools TV: it was coming up to Easter, apparently, though if you didn't live in their bright world of certainties you wouldn't know. In that world, it seemed, Easter was when people got baptised. Quite a happy-clappy occasion it looked nowadays; the presenter compared old and new rituals, old and new vows. He raised the remote to thumb all the nonsense away. A phrase caught his attention:

a new one, or at least he hadn't come across it before. The glamour of evil. Very odd. He found himself thinking of Louise's early efforts at glamour, the off-message lipstick and blobby mascara of her bedsit days.

More pious scrubbed faces presented for baptism, more crass phrases for them to mouth. Do you renounce Satan? I do. Well, what else would they say? No, I'll hang on to him if you don't mind? Matthew laughed as a trendy vicar in open-necked shirt filled the screen, young and earnest. A lookalike for the minister at the crematorium. A flick of the remote sent him dwindling away.

A cup of coffee, a detective story from the pile on the table. It didn't grip him today, though it was a classic, locked room, revolver in the shrubbery, the kind he usually liked. He had tried the grim realistic sort, mean streets and screams in the dark, and tossed them aside after a page or two. 'You get enough of that in the papers,' he remarked to Margaret, who nodded at her sewing in the safe living-room.

He went over to the window and looked down again on the Merchant City in the clean March sun. The smooth ashlar walls, the weathercock shifting pale in a gleam of gold. This is where I live. My life is here. This is who I am now. He washed up the breakfast things, leaving the kitchen scoured and bright.

He thought of going for a stroll through the pedestrianised plazas, but when he looked out again the sky was black and a random shower had made the chess squares shine. Okay. Pass the time. Clear out the boxes. Silly, really. All of that should have been cleared up long ago.

After another hour he hadn't got much clearing done, but the repetitive lifting and laying, the little decisions, were helping the day along. All Louise's frying-pans and knives and forks he put in one pile to be carried through to the kitchen, united with the well-worn pots and sieves and casseroles from the south-side house. Louise's life and Matthew's, seamlessly together at last. The few trashy books in another pile, for the sitting-room shelves or Oxfam. The Tampax and the lacy nightie in the bedroom drawers.

At least I got her nightshirt off.

The thought was all it took. Great danger. Matthew groaned, got up, hobbled around, yearning towards the door for the sound of Louise's key in the lock. She might come home early. She might sense that she was needed. Louise, you don't know what you're doing. You should be here.

But she seldom came home for lunch and it became clear that she wasn't coming home today. He went into the kitchen and hunted through cupboards and drawers. He felt Margaret's hand over his on the rubbed handle of the wooden spoon, stirring a pan of soup, as she'd always done, as she ought to be doing now. Louise didn't seem to have a saucepan, or in the chaos of the boxes it hadn't yet come to light. Matthew shrugged himself into his coat and went out to get a sandwich.

After the drift of light rain an uncertain near-spring sunlight lay on the Merchant City and it glittered fresh and clean. A bright coffee-house supplied salad rolls to go, and he chose some exotic dark blend of coffee in a lidded polystyrene cup. Lifestyle! This is who I am! Chirpy young men and women queued beside him, and in the clear busy air he saw himself like them, ordering his own life, in control. He had to be in control. Margaret gone and Louise so different from Margaret. He couldn't depend on Louise.

I mustn't get to depend on Louise.

But this is the way, this will work. I can do this, he thought, organising his grasp of the sandwich-box and the coffee-cup, stepping out into the shining street.

SOUTH SIDE MURDER, the newly-posted billboard said.

It was the earliest edition of the evening paper, carrying hardly any news at all. What there was Matthew read shaking in the lift, juggling sandwiches and coffee and smudgy tabloid pages. A girl in her early twenties. Wasteground behind a disco. The disco was named; he'd seen the name in neon tubing, flashing across the south-side road. That was what they called it. What they meant was the Moon and Stars.

He went into the back room and plunged into the job of sorting and clearing, while his sandwiches dried out and his coffee grew cold.

He had certainly made inroads into the mass of stuff, reaching boxes he hadn't seen before. From the next one, as he pulled it towards him, came a dull chinking of earthenware loosely packed. He unwrapped a pierrot, a cute kitten, a little boy hugging a little girl. He had long since stopped actually seeing the ornaments on the living-room mantelpiece, but once in a while he had been dimly aware that a two-foot high giraffe now stood where a ballerina used to be. Margaret had evidently brought her stock of ornaments out in rotation like the Burrell Collection. In the long afternoons, in the ring-fenced quiet south-side house. Maybe hoping he'd notice. While he thought of other things. He was crying again.

He took the newly-discovered ornaments through in armfuls and set them up in the living-room wherever he could find a space. Really there was no space, but he made some, moving things to and fro on the mantelpiece, jamming the new arrivals in here and there. Dark and light patches under the plinths now made it extremely obvious that Louise hadn't dusted for weeks. He rubbed his sleeve over the dust, while something odd teased the back of his mind once more. He thought of getting a proper duster and cleaning up the living-room. No, that's her job. There's something else I have to do. He stood there looking at the last two ornaments in his hands, wondering what that might be.

They'd have to go on the coffee-table, though Louise wouldn't be too pleased when she brought in the supper-tray. Matthew made an artistic arrangement with a kitten and a puppy and an ashtray and the folded evening paper. SOUTH SIDE MURDER. Behind the Moon and Stars. They didn't go far.

While I was on the bus coming home, he thought. While the wifie was regaling the bus with the whole story, pruriently mouthing the dreadful words the girl and boy had used. It wasn't the whole story after all. Before I got home, the blonde girl was dead in the mud.

In the back room the box of Margaret's clothes was waiting for him, though Margaret wasn't there. Matthew held her quilted dressing-gown close, crying and sobbing. It's good for me. The doctor said. He reached out to the next box, where, as he remembered, the letters were.

But he couldn't find them. He pulled out the old shoes, the cutlery, the cologne. He hauled everything out and pulled up the base-flaps of the cardboard box, in case they'd slipped in there. He put everything back in, poking inside every shoe as he did so, shaking the crumpled packing paper till a dim scent filled the room.

Well, it's the wrong box. Boxes reared around him, full of Margaret's gentle tweeds, full of Louise's unexpected silk and lace. After his work and his crying he was deathly tired; he couldn't search any more. The sun had moved round and the back room was too hot now. An unseasonable bluebottle, deceived by the warmth, buzzed in the window-pane. He dragged himself to his feet; the double-glazed unit opened smoothly, but the stumbling bluebottle didn't understand it was free to go. Matthew leaned out to squash it, and saw the old alley below.

He had never looked out of this window before. The front windows had their view of the Merchant City with its clean wide streets and courts, the fresh glass frontages on old buildings saved in the nick of time, restored and sanitised. From here, on the other side, you saw the way it used to be.

A very old house with a turnpike stair, weeds sprouting between its massive blocks of stone, an actual tree rooted in the slates of its witch's-hat roof. A lane three feet wide, silted up with broken glass and condoms. Black walls and greasy grey paving. When the architects came to put a new face on the city, this is what they found. The darkness underneath.

Still here. Another sifting spring shower shaded the bright afternoon. The gulls cried from the old river and the south side beyond.

The lift sang and the door clicked as Louise came home.

She had a carton of milk to stow in the fridge and her umbrella to shake dry. By the time she reached the living-room Matthew was safely on the sofa with the paper on his knee. She came over for her kiss and cried 'Snap!', tossing her paper on top of his.

But hers was a later edition. ARREST IN SOUTH SIDE MURDER was the headline now.

'That didn't take long,' Matthew said, bemused.

'No, it's her boyfriend, I believe.'

'They wouldn't say that. They never say that.'

'No, well, it's all over the office, of course. Speed of light, I don't know how they do it.' She flicked at her hair in the mantelpiece mirror and Matthew saw her glance, frowning slightly, at the expanded population of kittens and pierrots. 'He walked into the police station covered in blood.'

'Now that they can't know.'

'Amazing how often they get it right.' She lifted a china puppy-dog, hesitated, put it back with a shrug.

'I was worried – ' He caught her eye in the mirror. He couldn't remember what he'd been going to say. Instead he said, 'I thought – I think I might have passed them last night. The girl and the murderer.'

'What, when you were getting your pizza?' She turned, laughing in surprise.

'I didn't get a pizza. I went to the south side,' Matthew said. 'I wanted to see our house again. Margaret's house. I used to feel safe there.'

He cried himself out this time with his head in Louise's breasts. Silk skin and lilac sweetness, but not a stir. It's working. This is what I need.

'It's why – ' he sobbed, ' – it's why I brought out the ornaments.' Of course that simply sounded silly and he wasn't sure she understood. She couldn't understand. 'In memory of Margaret,' he wept. It was as near as he could go.

Her gentle hand smoothed his hair and his damp face. 'That need will pass,' said her voice far above his head.

'It won't!' he screamed. He jerked upright and for a moment they stared at each other. Frightened. Both.

'I was worried,' he said at last, 'in case I was there.'

She blinked at him.

'It was a terrible feeling, Louise. To think I might have been there. When the girl was murdered.' High heels and velvet hat. Golden hair draggled in the muddy desolation behind the Moon and Stars. 'I might have been passing. At the very time.'

'Spooky,' she said, too lightly. She didn't understand. 'And they might have wanted you as a witness, I suppose.'

'They wouldn't need me,' he sniffled. 'There was a wifie at the bus stop who saw everything I saw.'

Louise laughed again at that, shifting in the chair, rubbing her leg where he leaned heavy on her. 'There's always a wifie, isn't there?' She took his shoulders gently and held him off, glancing at the clock.

He wasn't in any way prepared for the flood of cold rage that left him shaking. 'I'm not *boring* you, am I?'

'Oh Matthew.' She held him close again, caring for him.

This is what I need.

No. I need more.

He fought it down. Thought of Margaret. The rage ebbed and so did he. Louise, in motherly mode, was stroking his cheek and hair. 'There now, love. Whatever can we find for you to do all day?'

'The boxes,' he muttered.

'Well, yes, not quite a second career.'

'I found some of Margaret's clothes,' he suddenly said.

'Better throw these out.' She wasn't as certain as she sounded. He caught the worried flicker in her eyes. 'You should get out more,' she said, 'to coin a phrase. You could learn to drive.'

'Should have learned long ago.' Why hadn't he? 'It wasn't that common then.'

'When you lived with your mum. I know.' Definitely looking at the clock now. 'And after that Margaret did the driving, I suppose.'

'She was glad to.' But Louise had wriggled out of his arms and stood up, while his thoughts spun free, out of gear. 'I could have learned,' he said. 'If we'd just got it organised. Margaret never seemed to think it was the right time. Where are you going, Louise?'

She was making for the shower. 'Office party. Remember?'

'Oh God, I'm not in the mood.'

'We needn't stay long.' She stood in the doorway, unstrapping her watch, hopping to take off her shoes. 'I'm not sure it will be quite your thing.'

'But we're going anyway, are we?' he said to the closed bathroom door.

They hadn't had a shower in the south-side house until a few years ago. The time he was remembering was long before that.

Margaret in the bath. Gentle splashing and swishing. From nowhere, in the middle of the evening, the need came on. He drew back the plushy curtain and looked out into the south-side night. Above the garden trees there was a single star.

He croaked Margaret's name.

He knew it was Louise splashing in the shower, not Margaret in the bath, but the door opened and out she came, huddled in one of their wedding-present towels, almost threadbare now after all those happy south-side years. 'Margaret,' he said. 'You've got to look after me.'

She dropped the towel and held out her arms. He backed her into the bathroom, in all the dampness and scented steam. New fittings, ceramic tiles, so it was easy, when they'd finished, to mop any stains away.

5

Really this is my first ever party, he thought in the hot buzzing room. Never went to parties with Margaret. Before Margaret, of course, there wasn't the chance.

I'll give you something to cry for.

No.

First ever party, and the trouble was, it showed. Louise had introduced him to a couple of people, but no conversation of any length ensued. 'Nice talking to you, Matthew,' they said, and went off to talk to somebody else. Some of the guests were from other companies, so that they didn't even know Louise. They certainly didn't want to know Louise's spouse. Matthew stood alone studying the display boards of press cuttings, photographs, congratulatory letters, for half an hour at least. He could have written a dissertation on Louise's fucking firm, if any of the information from the boards had managed to get past the angry misery in his brain.

And Louise? Wasn't it supposed to be a new life for her too?

She was having the proverbial ball. Executive lady, corporate woman; he'd never seen her like this before. She had made a grand entrance, rustling in her stiff silk skirts shot with black and red; she applauded the chairman's bum-numbingly boring conspectus of the last ten years; she raised her glass to his achievement, no, the achievement of each and every person here. As if it mattered. As if it was a life and death thing.

Drained that glass. Picked up another from a circulating tray. Didn't take long to knock that one off. No wonder she was talking and laughing fluently as she moved from group to group of flushed faces and damp eyes. Behind the laugh there was a constant pussycat smile, letting people know that he had – that they'd –

He shook himself. Come on! New life! On the south side it was routine, twice a week, in bed with the light out. Here in the Merchant City, forget the rules. Half the couples here probably – Before they came out –

He felt the bathroom tiles on his bare skin, slick with Louise's talcum powder, cold and wrong.

Across the room, against the dark glass of the window, looking down into the street where bright beetles ran, stood a tall blonde girl, alone.

No. Not in the Merchant City. It won't happen here.

Louise laughed, wide-mouthed, in a group of friends. She ought to be looking after me. Margaret did. Can't expect Margaret here.

As at the funeral, he looked for her all the same, tears in his eyes. There she was. At the funeral she had turned out to be Louise, but not tonight, because there was Louise giggling by the buffet table, and there was Margaret standing beside the blonde girl.

Knowing she has to look after me.

On the other side of the blonde girl now was her partner, a morose ugly bugger in a pale grey suit, a shortarse, hardly up to her square shoulder. Beyond her, mirrored against the street of lighted windows, Louise.

'Hell of a change you've made in Louise!' said somebody under his nose. Matthew blinked and came back from where he'd been.

Somebody speaking directly to him; he'd nearly forgotten such a thing could be. Small guy, well on in drink, garlic dip on his expensive hand-stitched lapels. 'You're Matthew, yeah? You're Louise's husband?' the small guy said.

'No, she's my wife.'

But he couldn't really have said that, because the small guy was blethering on. 'Naw, congratulations, she's blossomed. When was it you got married again?'

'First of December. Three months ago. To the day.' Across the room she was all but fucking the chairman, his shy bride.

More congratulations from the wee pissed guy. 'Three bastarn months! What a change! We've all tried to get into - ' Drunk but not that drunk, he managed to steer into slightly more decorous waters: 'Get her to let her hair down. No chance. Don't mind me saying, Matthew?'

'No, that's okay, mate.'

No chance, well, no wonder, for this pallid skelf, chest-high to Matthew, liable to get lost on his way up to Louise's knee. But across the room she was raising her face to laugh into the black eyes of a big smoothie with equally cultured lapels and a lot more hair. 'That one tried,' the small guy confirmed. 'Hearts and flowers and valentine cards. God knows why he kept at it, no, I don't mean that, no offence, Matthew. But le major knockback every time.'

'Known Louise for a while, have you?'

'Thass what I'm saying, Matthew.' Little arm waving at the display boards, slopping red wine to join the garlic dip. 'Every year! Party! Skeleton at the feast! Don't mind me saying, do you?'

'No. Cheers.'

He looked properly at the photographs for the first time. Group after group, year by year, with Louise hovering pale and shy on the outer fringe. This year, life and soul of the party, as she would say herself. He stared in some wonder across the room.

'Whatcha do to her, Matthew? Naw, don't get me wrong, I mean, whatcha do?'

Not much. That's the odd thing.

To divert the little yapper's train of thought Matthew scanned the photographs again. 'How long has she been with the firm then?'

'*I* dunno!' In his liquefied redoubt the little drunk guy took obscure offence. 'Five years maybe. *I* dunno. Do you not know?'

'Oh yes, five years, that's about right.'

But he didn't know. He ought to know.

He knew two things about Louise, he realised. Or two halves of the same thing. Until the moment when she turned up at Margaret's funeral, he didn't know anything else about her at all. One: she'd been Margaret's best friend. Two: Margaret had written letters to her. A great many letters.

Three. He couldn't find those letters now.

Across the room she was laughing again with the careless freedom of the truly blotto. Matthew heard her but couldn't see her behind the ranks of chattering women and swaying men. Her friends; did they know all about her? From the little guy's maunderings, he doubted it. They didn't know anything about her, or about him. Nor about their marriage. But then nobody was allowed to know that.

He looked for the blonde girl but she wasn't there. A door stood open, where she and her monkey-faced partner could have slipped through. What were they doing now?

He looked for Margaret. He looked, without much hope, for Louise.

Nobody noticed how often he went to the gents. With these expeditions, and further close study of the photograph boards, and a bit of soulful staring over the bobbing heads that totally ignored him, he managed to pass the evening, and at last it was time to go home. More than time; they were almost the last to leave. He stared coldly at Louise when she fetched up at his side, grabbing his arm, pissed as a whole vivarium.

'Had a good evening, have you?' he enquired.

'Great! The best! And you?' But she didn't listen to his reply. She wasn't looking after him. Hadn't all evening. Couldn't now. She couldn't bite her finger, let alone look after him.

I will never be angry with Louise.

As they rode down in the glass lift Matthew stood aloof. On their left, Merchant City lifestyle worn with panache, stood a pair of gay men happily holding hands. On their right was the leggy blonde girl. Lipstick on her partner's smooth grey shoulder. An ear-ring she had to refix under the sweeping hair.

In the foyer a new problem arose. 'Louise, you can't drive home.'

'Course I can, silly boy.' To prove it she evidently intended to flourish her car keys, but the enterprise ran into trouble when she couldn't open her handbag. 'Oh sugar. You drive. No, hang on, you can't, can you? That won't work.' She furrowed her brow as if she was still capable of thought.

'Come on, we'll get a taxi. You can pick up the car tomorrow.' Matthew steered her into the quiet Merchant City square.

Quiet? That'll be right! The remaining party-goers spilled out behind them, and it was evidently chucking-out time for all the city-centre pubs and clubs too. Cruising taxis converged on the scene. Matthew lifted his hand, but under his elbow there was a darting little grey marmoset: the small bastard, dragging his long-legged blonde behind him. Into the taxi. Into the dark close box, together.

Not a taxi. No.

Louise was trying to hail one, but the drivers refused to see her, no matter how much she capered and waved. 'Look,' Matthew said, since people were beginning to giggle around them, 'we'll walk. It's no distance after all.' The Merchant City lifestyle, that's what it's all about, a short walk from all amenities with a drunken gambolling wife on your arm.

When they had been walking for a minute or two, she did quieten down. The wide chessboard streets, the clean-cut walls. A full moon rode high and the shadows were strange. Louise's heels rang echoes from the buildings on either side. Danger. No, this is Louise.

He pulled her close to him, soft crushable breasts under the stiff silk and the warm mohair wrap. All her powder and scent and deodorant and anti-perspirant had washed away. He smelled excited sweat, an old smell that he knew.

A single star. No. No.

'Where we going, eh, Matthew?'

'Home. Quick as we can. It's time you were in bed.'

'Can't wait.' A giggle and a shiver within his circling arm.

'That's why I'm taking you this way. This is a short cut.'

It was the alley behind the flats. He knew it by the old house, poking its pointy roof above the clean gentrified sandstone, under the riding moon.

Moon-shadows in the alley. In the shadow of the turnpike stair they stopped for a kiss. Danger. No, none, for it was Louise's sweat in his nostrils, Louise grinding and pressing and panting in his arms. If she'd been drunk before she was miraculous now. His shirt was ripped open and her little ferret teeth got to work. Matthew found a zip and her cushiony breasts spilled out whiter than the moon. He knelt in the mud and nuzzled through silk and lace, uncovering her paleness in the moon-shadows beneath the dripping old wall.

'What, here?' she gasped.

'Why not?'

She giggled. 'Very naughty smack bottom,' she said, so he did until she kicked and crowed with joy. He followed it up, couldn't stop now, thumping away till the house-walls rang. She flung her arms wide in ecstasy, then gripped him, and the moon exploded.

Must have. It was gone. But its cold light still sifted down on Matthew and Louise where they squirmed on the sodden stone. It was only a leaning chimney-head that had blocked out, from where he lay, the full passionless disc in the sky. When he sat up it swam back into view.

Louise was sprawled in the filthy alley, eyes closed, her dress pulled off her shoulders, skirts up, pants tangled round her shoes. The bleaching moonlight took the colour from her hair.

It isn't finished yet.

She opened big wide eyes and smiled at him like a cat. 'Oh wow,' she said. She reached out to him, but he was already standing up, zipping and shaking himself into place. She scrambled to her feet with no helping hand, sorted her pants and tights, wriggled her dress straight, found her handbag abandoned in the muck. She cuddled up to him, butting her head into his chest. Her hair smelt of old dead things.

'You'll be wanting a shower now,' he said.

'And you! You stink!' Stars in her eyes. 'Let's save water,' she said, 'get in together and then - '

The electric charge between them was strong as death. Not finished yet.

'You go on,' he said. 'I won't be long. Think I need to cool down a bit.'

'Don't cool down too far,' she called behind him as he strode off down the alley towards the south side.

6

No buses, of course, at this time of night, but he would have walked anyway, deep into the unfolding layers of the south side. Over the bridge where the sleepy water sucked away. Down the long street leading south, its blackened tenements flickering into clear view and then away as running clouds crossed and recrossed the moon. In the triangle between the two roads, he knew, chimneys split the sky with roaring flame. When he turned his head to look at them they weren't there.

The tenements were there, with a headscarfed wifie shuffling into a dark close. At this time of night? He paused for a moment, but yes, she was really there.

And the dance-hall was there. No, the disco. No, it was the dance-hall, the Moon and Stars, with the zodiac arching above its door. Matthew walked past it and heard his footsteps ring from the flat facade. A real full moon tonight. Sometimes a moon. At other times a single star.

One, two, three.

He looked back as if the blonde girl and her boyfriend might still be quarrelling there. He thought he could see the police tapes fluttering round the wasteground where she lay. Had lain. Would lie.

The old tenements were silent under the moon. Nobody about, you wouldn't expect it; not after a murder, even with a confession and a bloodstained boy locked in a cell. They remembered too well. As he remembered the tall tenements and the black closemouths, so they remembered him.

He knew she'd come. It was that sort of night.

He knew where he would see her, in the last patch of light before the dance-hall cast its shadow, and there she was, a blonde girl walking home. Heading for the tenements, but she wasn't going to get there. Knowing that, he stood, no hurry, up against the wall, drinking in every detail.

She looked round once or twice. A girl on her own, they always did. Short hair, smartly cut, a cap of gleaming gold. He knew he was indistinct against the damp-patched stone in the shifting, staining light, and she didn't see him. He was nearer than her nightmares. Last lap. Now.

The full moon swam free of cloud above the chimneys, bright as a halogen lamp. He saw her in total clarity, and she saw him. They were both shocked into paralysis, but her young synapses recovered first. She was off like a whippet and she had her keys in her hand.

She had to get through the close before she was safe. The famous tenement close, the common passageway, welcoming to all. Open to all. He was three paces behind her and he would have her before she got to the stairs.

But this was a different city, a different world.

He heard a distinctive bang and click, and pulled up in front of a slammed security door. A strong lock and wired glass. Sharp heels ran up stone stairs, a key turned, a door flew open, and finally a storm door crashed shut, a slab of varnished wood that had stood impregnable for a hundred years. He'd never had to deal with any of that before.

He imagined, though of course he couldn't hear, telephone wires shimmering with sound under the clear-eyed moon.

As in a dream he saw a bus coming, a lighted galleon, taking him away. He raced across the road to catch it and sat down. Calmly now, don't attract attention; he got out his fare ready for the conductor, but the driver was roaring at him, he'd done something wrong. And he knew it was a dream, because the money was all wrong, light in his palm like holiday centimes. He stared at it in horror, looking for sixpence or threepence or even half-a-crown.

'How faur you gaun?' the driver seemed to want to know.

'City centre,' he whimpered.

'Sixty-five pee.' It made no sense at all.

A young man, clattering downstairs ready to get off, leaned over and picked out some of the tinny change, stuck it in a slot and put a ticket in his hand. Things shook and shivered and settled into place. They think I'm drunk, Matthew realised. Legless: as he flopped into the nearest seat he might as well have been. He did remember drinking quite a lot of wine. The party. Louise.

'Okay now, John?' said the kind young man.

Jim or John, whatever. 'Yeah, cheers, pal.' He sat tight in the seat dedicated to the elderly, sick and infirm, remembering something else. Nothing else. No.

The cool ashlar courtyards of the Merchant City drew him in; in through the glass doors, across the foyer, up in the whispering lift. Louise had left a dimmed lamp in the hall and light glimmered from the bedroom, but the smooth hill of the duvet didn't move and she didn't call to him. He went and had a shower, turning the water up as hot as it would go, soaping every inch until he was a statue in white foam. Then the long scalding fingers jetting it all away. He stood in the steamy bathroom towelling himself dry. I will never hurt Louise.

But he needed her, as he had needed Margaret many a time. He crossed the hall at an awkward run. A drift of apple-blossom scent met him on the threshold and he knew it would be all right. It always had been. A flash, as if he didn't have enough to put up with, of a sweaty young body hot from dancing; but none of that here. A clean bed and Margaret, asleep. He needed her, but only in a husbandly way. Conjugal rights. Quietly, politely, did you enjoy that? Then he could sleep. He turned back the quilt and blankets to slip into the humdrum marriage bed.

Margaret's eyes were open. She knew where he had been.

Her lips parted. She was going to say something. But she never did. What she was going to say mustn't be said.

'I can't help it,' he begged.

And it was Louise in the bed. Eyes open, twinkling, taking him all in. 'Hey! You haven't had enough, have you?' she said.

Matthew grabbed for her nightshirt but found sweet-scented flesh instead. Naked, she pounced on him, rolled over him, spreadeagled, soft. He rolled her back. What he did was only what a husband would do.

She screamed in joy; she loved it, she joined in with abandon as he bit and thrust and banged. When he finally lay back he knew he'd have bruises in the morning too. Louise lay sprawled over the covers, smiling, blissfully asleep. Apple-blossom hung around them. Great danger here.

7

It occurred to Matthew one day that the pierrots had disappeared from the mantelpiece. He hadn't seen them go.

Well, Louise had been moving things about. But the pierrots hadn't just been moved, they were nowhere to be seen. Looking round, he realised that the living-room was nearly clear of ornaments. Just a couple of shepherd-boys on the coffee-table, where at one time there had been a perfect menagerie of kittens and giraffes.

So she had moved some of them back to the boxes. Sensible girl. He supposed he had brought rather too many through. Hard to remember now, that dusty sunny day in the back room, crying over Margaret fit to break his heart. Stumbling through with his silly arms full of giraffes. He'd hardly thought about Margaret since. It was passing, as everybody said it would.

Since the office party there had been a quiet spell, apparently, at Louise's work. Ten days, two weeks perhaps? A lull in launches and client meetings, or anyway Louise hadn't had to go to them. There had been some pleasant evenings at home, just Matthew and Louise side by side on the sofa watching TV. Then off to bed. He smiled to himself. And Louise becoming almost houseproud. Moving things round.

Not checking on the pierrots, of course not, he crossed the hall into the back room. Louise had dug out the full-length mirror from her bedsit and hung it in the hallway. Another small change. It made the narrow space look bigger, opened it out: a brighter, airier place, not quite the same.

Far fewer boxes in the back room than there used to be.

Nothing wrong with that. He had cleared out stuff himself, hadn't he, pots and pans to the kitchen, books to the living-room shelves, nighties to the bedside drawers? Louise had only carried that process on. The box with Margaret's clothes was still there. Nearest the door. In the long last week, in the hospital, Margaret's bed had been nearest the door of the ward; the patient next expected to go.

The two or three boxes remaining were stacked along one wall. The floor had been swept and the window rubbed clean, at least in parts; corporate woman in a struggle for survival, perhaps, with the new housewifely Louise. He peered through the fly-spotted pane at the ancient house in the alley, positively picturesque in the spring sun. The tree rooted in its slates was showing an unexpected splash of green. He looked down at the greasy cobbles where Louise had tossed and screamed. Ten days, two weeks ago?

Back in the living-room he couldn't quite get comfortable on the sofa, and something was making him want to sneeze. He tracked it down to a vase of wilting daffodils at the window, spilling their pollen on the sill. That had been one of Louise's briskest days, setting the vase on the windowsill, dusting the blond wood till it shone. Old newspapers had been stacked into tidy bundles, even if they hadn't yet quite made it to the bin. The pierrot-free mantelpiece had been dusted too. Louise had even twitched at Margaret's red velvet curtains, speaking of getting new ones soon. He told her quite sharply that they had years of wear left in them yet.

He wriggled on the sofa, packing cushions behind his spine. It didn't work. Not enough cushions. Margaret's big red velvet cushions, like the pierrots, had disappeared.

She sat on the sofa beside him with her sewing on her lap. But she didn't. She wasn't there. Blink and screw up his eyes as he might, she wouldn't come.

'It happens,' the minister said. 'It means you don't need her now.' Matthew thumbed the remote to switch on the television but then he couldn't see it for tears.

Louise came breezing in with a load of delicatessen bags. Since it was spring, she had thrown off her scarves and heavy coat and her sturdy black legs were visible now. She leaned over for a quick kiss and he caught a new lemony scent. Unless that came from the plastic bags. He reached up to give her a hug, though there was rather less for him to nuzzle around her soft hips and thighs. She was off into the kitchen before he could ask for more.

He followed her to the cooker. Even the kitchen, he realised, was less cluttered than it used to be. He saw the coffee-café-kaffee mugs, but none of Margaret's flower-scattered cups and saucers, cream-jugs, sugar-bowls. Louise, already started on her chopping and slicing for dinner, looked up but didn't smile at him. Very quick kiss, that had been.

'Louise – ' he said. But what did he want to say? Please stop dusting the mantelpiece? What he settled on sounded just as silly: 'Where have all the cushions gone?'

'Try it again with music.' She smiled, but it wasn't much of a smile.

He couldn't read her. Like the mirrored hallway, she was strange. 'What is it, Louise?'

She sighed, tipping vegetables into a pan, adjusting a switch, stirring with care. 'There's something in the evening paper. I didn't know whether to tell you,' she said. Or Margaret said.

Matthew stood like stone. An evening paper lying on the coffee-table beside the china dogs. Margaret at the window looking out, fingering the velvet curtain, her back to him. 'I thought you might know already.'

'How would I know?' He'd binned the paper. Or Margaret had. He'd never seen it again.

'Well, on the afternoon news,' Louise was saying.

'I didn't see the news.'

Another sigh as she wiped her hands on a dishcloth. She never wore an apron and she was still in her office blouse and skirt. 'I'm sorry, Matthew. This is going to be a shock to you,' she said.

She disentangled the evening paper from the ciabatta and olives in her shopping-bag, but he stared at the black print for long minutes before he was able to make out the words. The next-door neighbours, not the ones with the blonde daughter, the couple on the other side. He hardly ever saw them: the south side was like that. But he must have seen their garage, a carbon copy of Margaret's, the minimal single-car lock-up tucked in beside the house. Must have seen the car in which they had seated themselves side by side, deep-breathing exhaust fumes.

The blonde daughter, walking home late, had spotted something wrong. He saw her crooking her long back, straddling her long legs, to peer through a crack in the garage doors. He heard her cough and sob as she ran for help, wiping her red eyes with a thin young hand.

Louise steered him back into the living-room, poured drinks, curled up beside him on the sofa. She took her shoes off and burrowed her black toes under a cushion: a green cushion that he had never seen before. He wanted red velvet and Margaret.

Red velvet and Margaret. Would that be enough?

'Did you know them well, love?' Louise was saying.

'Hardly at all. High hedges.' The south-side hedges that kept you safe. Used to keep you safe. 'The girl who found them, you saw her at the funeral. She was coming back from a dance. Met death like that,' he said, and bit the heel of his hand.

Louise drew him close and comforted him. That's what she was there for, after all.

Another drink. Tears wiped from Matthew's eyes, and sympathetic tears from Louise's. 'They just look so ordinary,' she was saying, staring at the photograph in the paper. Plain smiling faces in a snatched party snap. 'So ordinary,' a sad wonder in her tone. 'What's going on in their minds?'

'You can never tell that.'

She maundered on. 'They could have been planning it already. There, at a party, with people all around. They could have been planning to die.'

'In our street. Our bit of the south side.'

'It can happen anywhere, to anyone, Matthew, love.'

'But it was safe there.' He tried to explain, because she had to understand. 'Some places are safe.' He pulled her desperately into him and buried his face between her breasts. 'Margaret kept me safe,' he whispered in the warm scented cave.

'I know. She told me.'

Matthew couldn't look up, couldn't breathe.

'She worried a lot,' Louise said above his head, 'about what would happen if she was the first to die. What you'd do. It was as if she knew - '

Louise isn't Margaret. He tried one last time. 'That's why I brought the whole house here,' he whispered. 'The carpets and curtains. The ornaments. The sofa and the chairs.'

'Yes, I know,' Louise was saying again. He didn't dare to look. Didn't have to. One hand still stroked him in an absent comforting way, but she was doing something quite different with the other one. Several things. 'You missed Margaret so much. But that will pass,' she was breathing in his ear.

She slipped a strap, opened a clip, wriggled and eased till her beautiful breasts fell free. The hand was busy again. 'Now we have a proper marriage,' she murmured. 'Haven't we?'

Louise uptight in her flat, perched on a straight chair, embarrassed if he even had to go to the loo. Louise in her first weeks as a bride, showering and powdering both before and after the act. This wasn't that Louise. Danger. But she was soft as a cushion, velvet-warm, and he couldn't stop himself. Absolutely nothing he could do.

'Oh bugger,' Louise said. 'We seem to have overdone it slightly.'

He stared in horror at the sofa. Margaret's sofa. 'That never, never happened before,' he said.

Louise briskly moved a cushion to cover the stain. 'Never mind,' she said. 'It's seen its best days.'

'You wouldn't throw it out? Margaret's sofa?' he said in alarm.

'Would I do that, Matthew?' She wasn't laughing, was she? She hadn't answered, he realised as she slid off his knee and pattered barefoot through the hall. He heard the toilet flush and the hot water run. Wound up as he was, he heard, impossibly, the soft puff of talcum powder in the secret corners he knew.

'No, but I meant to tell you,' her voice floated back, and she reappeared with a bulging paper parcel in her arms. He had seen it, without noticing, among the boxes in the back room. 'Picked up some curtain material the other day. Look, isn't it bliss? Bedroom, spare room, and then I thought for this room –'

She ripped open the thin paper wrapping over a length of furnishing material, no, three lengths, in three different patterns that toned in together, shades of green and brown like young willow trees. The price-tags made Matthew blink. Can't be right. Margaret never spent money like that. Three rooms at once! Three rooms in the same cool colours. Louise's rooms.

'See? What d'you think?' she was saying. 'Next to these curtains? Honestly now, will they do? The sofa and the chairs?' Acting the haberdasher, she flung the material out in a greeny-browny wave. A thick folded corner caught the horns of one remaining china giraffe, awkwardly sited on the coffee-table. Of course it crashed against the wall. Of course its long fragile neck shattered into fragments, never to be repaired.

'Oh God!' screeched Louise. Unbelievably, he realised, it was a screech of laughter. She doubled up, hooting, tears of mirth in her eyes.

I'll give you something to cry about. He reached out for her as the hands of the clock stood still.

She was up and away. 'Oh God!' again, still laughing, as she slapped the oven-timer to silence its piercing scream. She bent over the oven and her little short skirt rode up. She had nothing on below.

He hung in deep space where Margaret had never gone. She'd gone to the loo but she hadn't put her pants back on. Ready and willing, shy Louise. She never used to be. She shouldn't be. She's changed and the house is changing. Great danger. It isn't finished yet.

'Another five minutes and it'd have been ruined.' She had knotted up her hair so that it didn't trail in the sauce, and she was flitting about the kitchen from cooker to table to built-in cupboard, a real little housewife among her pots and pans. Barefoot, of course, no reason why not in the centrally-heated flat. Margaret moving calmly in the cavernous south-side kitchen, sometimes in boots and socks when the elderly radiators broke down. Always in an apron. Under the apron a tweed skirt and a petticoat and a girdle and knickers and bra, safely holding her, and him too, for thirty years. Louise bent to the oven again and he could see her bare bottom. As she must know.

'Here we are!' she cried merrily, turning to face him with a scalding-hot casserole in her hands, between herself and him.

I will never be angry with Louise.

'One of my best, yeah?' she remarked modestly as they mopped up the last of the sauce. He thought back to casseroles Margaret had made, none as flavoursome as this. After the meal the table-clearing, the washing-up, the long safe evening in mahogany and crimson peace. Decorous bed at half-past ten. That's how it used to be.

They moved back into the living-room for coffee. 'Early night tonight?' he suggested.

'I wish,' she said, 'but I'm going out tonight. Oh God, look at the *time*!'

He couldn't believe it, but she was up and scampering around, clapping down a cup of instant coffee for him, running between bathroom and bedroom, dropping her blouse here and her skirt there. By the time he caught up, she had wriggled into a skimpy red dress and was doing up her big doe-eyes. 'It's the launch of the new thing, I'm sure I told you. Might be a bit late,' she said into the dressing-table mirror, 'you won't mind?'

'You never told me.'

'Didn't I? Thought I had.' She put down the mascara and picked up the blusher. 'Anyway I didn't think you'd want to come.'

'You might have asked at least.'

'Oh Matthew, you *never* want to come. And it's business, I've got to be there.' She was concentrating on her cheekbones with just the occasional glance over her shoulder at him, but his stormy silence must have got through. 'Look, love, I made your dinner, didn't I? And we had quite a good tumble, didn't we? You can last out surely till I come back.'

'Quite good?' he said.

Her laugh this time was a bit nervous. So well it might be. But she put on a cheeky front, as if everything was fine: 'Not bad. So what's the problem?'

I will never be angry with Louise.

'I'll show you what's the problem.' he said.

He wasn't angry and she even giggled at first, sprawled over his knee, thinking it was all a bit of fun. He whipped her until she knew it wasn't a joke and then turned her on to the bed, following on down. He thought, in the brief moment he had to think, that she did look shocked this time. Or excited. He wasn't excited and he wasn't angry, doing only what a husband had to do. She was excited. He felt her shudder and heard her cry.

He sat back, panting, on his heels. 'Not bad?' he said.

Her mascara was all over her face and her lipstick crazily splotched. She swallowed once or twice. 'Did you ever do that to Margaret?' she said.

He didn't quite understand. 'Of course,' he said. 'She was my wife.'

'Yes. Okay.' She sat up among the rags of her dress and underclothes. 'I'll have to find something else to wear.' She looked a bit warily at him, as if that might annoy him again.

'That little black frock's nice,' he said.

He went back to his congealed cup of coffee in the living-room. Did you ever do that to Margaret? Just once. She saw to that, sitting up bruised on the floor. He didn't meet her eyes. Pulling herself on to the sofa, where she sat upright as a judge. 'Matthew,' she said, 'if you ever do that again, I think you know what I'll do.'

Louise was coming through the hall, dressed in the little black frock, make-up in place. She looked at herself as she passed the full-length mirror, head to toe. Like the flat, she was cool and strange. As she walked right up to him, he said 'Margaret understood.' As near to an apology as he could go.

'Did she now?' said Louise.

She took him by the shoulders, as she had done in the hall of her bedsit. As unexpectedly, as fiercely as then. A tiger kiss, thrusting at him till he seized her again. No apology required. He felt her high excitement. High and very strange.

'Oh fuck,' she said, 'look at the time,' and she whisked away from him. She moved so fast. Bag, coat, car keys; he heard the door bang and the lift whisper down.

The living-room melted around him, shifting and reforming to Louise's design. Bad things can happen in safe places. In the Merchant City? He pushed that thought away and looked for Margaret. Since it wasn't her living-room any more, she wasn't there.

No. All right. That happens. I don't need her any more. The minister said.

I will never be angry with Margaret. No, Louise.

I didn't get angry. It isn't finished yet.

The flat was alien, the kitchen was alien, microwave and dishwasher, Louise's casseroles and wooden spoons. In the fresh pale hall with the full-length mirror he saw his reflection, slightly different, like Louise. Somehow a younger man.

It isn't finished yet. He went down in the lift, crossed the shining courtyard, and turned towards the south side, following an old routine.

8

Matthew woke in the clear Merchant City morning air and realised that he had slept extremely well.

He had been late coming in. He remembered staring at the hands of the clock, not believing what it seemed to say. But Louise was later still, and he had been long in bed, lying open-eyed in the dark, when he heard her key stuttering in the door. He turned over and fell into a deep sleep.

So he was alert enough at breakfast, but Louise was morose. She crawled out of bed and swallowed painkillers; at the table she pushed muesli sickly around her bowl. 'Had a good time, did you?' he said.

'We went on to a club.' Together with her white face and panda eyes, that seemed to answer that.

'Are you going out tonight?'

'No.' He thought there might be more to come. She saw him looking at her. 'Never going out again,' she offered with an attempt at a laugh. But that wasn't what she had been about to say.

'Good,' he said. 'I don't like it when you go out.'

'Oh for God's sake, Matthew!' she yelled.

That evidently hurt her head. She linked her fingers together to cradle her fragile brow, but went determinedly on. 'What is it with you? Surely to God you can make your own supper once in a while?'

'It's not that.' He knew it wasn't. What was it, though?

'What is it then?'

'I don't like it when you're out in the city,' he said, 'on your own. It isn't a nice place, Louise. You might - you might get into trouble.'

'Oh Matthew,' she sighed. 'I drive from here to there. I keep my doors locked. I've got a bloody mobile, I'd phone if –' She poured coffee, slopping it over the rim of the mug. She dabbed it up and licked her wrist where it had splashed the skin. She looked up, straight at him for a moment. 'Margaret never went out without you, did she?' she said.

'Hardly ever. And I never went out without her.' Why had he said that? There was a reason, he knew.

'That must have been fun.' But she wasn't paying attention; a glance at the clock, a trawl under the table for her shoes. She wasn't *listening*. She looked startled as he slid along the breakfast bench. 'Don't go yet,' he said. 'I want you to understand.'

She was trying to get up from the table. Matthew helped her, hoisting her to her feet, his hands hard under her armpits. He walked her backwards through the hall and into the living-room. 'Things happen and they worry me,' he said. 'Margaret used to look after me. It's absolutely essential that you should look after me now.'

'I do try.' She was backed up against the sofa by this time.

'Show me how.'

'Matthew, I'll be late for work.'

'If you are,' he said, 'you can tell them why.' Unexpectedly he saw a glimmer in her eye and he followed that theme through, saying 'This is better than work, isn't it?' as he did the things she liked him to do.

Louise, tight-lipped, pushed him aside. 'Look, Matthew, cut it out, okay? I'm not Margaret.' He knew it was the hangover speaking, but still it hurt. 'Margaret had all day for this but I don't. You'll have to get used to that.' Car keys, jacket, and the front door banged.

I will never be angry with Louise.

When he next looked at the clock, most of the morning had gone. 'That can't be right,' he said to the empty room.

And it wasn't, because the hands moved anti-clockwise to the time he wanted it to be. Margaret, standing beside him, had done that. 'I thought you'd gone,' he said, and tears of relief pricked his eyes. He felt the warm rub of her jersey sleeve against his arm, he could see its coarse ribbing, the occasional stitch she had dropped. 'I thought I didn't need you any more. But I do.'

The clock wasn't making sense, but he got a time-check on the radio, snapping it off before the news began. A good part of the day still stretched ahead, and he had nothing in mind to do. He thought he wouldn't go out and get a paper today.

'I never went out without you, Margaret,' he said in the hall.

'Yes, you did,' he heard her say in the kitchen behind him. He spun round, but she wasn't there. Face to face she wouldn't speak. Never had.

He went into the bedroom and pulled open the drawers where Louise kept her knickers and tights, upending everything on the bed. He felt around the carcase of the tallboy in case anything had slipped into another drawer. He attacked the built-in wardrobe and flailed among Louise's coats and jackets, searched the pockets, opened the bags, pushed his fingers into the toes of the shoes. Not there.

'What are you looking for, Matthew?' Margaret said.

He knew she knew the answer.

'Why?' he heard her say.

The bedroom was a disaster area by now. Soberly he tidied up the drawers and shelves and went back into the living-room. Margaret was sitting on the sofa, big red velvet cushions nested around. She had pushed the pierrots to one side and, stooped over the little table, she was writing a letter to her faraway friend Louise. Her thin wrist curved round the paper and he couldn't see what she was writing, didn't know. He wept in frustration because he couldn't see.

He made more coffee, sharp in the appetite now. He crunched up buttered toast and spun the dial of the radio from music to sport to vapid chat. A news bulletin came on and he stood stock-still to listen, but it was only two minutes long. Music, sport, chatter again. He rinsed the breakfast dishes and stacked them up to dry. At the coat-hooks in the hall he couldn't find his jacket, though he'd gone out wearing it last night.

The quilted winter jacket he eventually put on was a mistake, because out in the shining Merchant City genuine sunshine was lapping the cliffs of glass and stone. He was the only man in winter gear among butterfly dresses and coloured shirts. He pulled off his jacket and slung it over his shoulder by one finger. See me, I'm trendy! But a coldness lay on his skin.

He bought a paper and found a vacant bench, with some difficulty, since everyone else seemed to think that spring had come. He sat down and raised his face to the warm deceiving sun. Still cold.

He read the paper, which didn't tell him much that he didn't already know.

Lovely day for a walk. Plenty of buses at this time, but he thought he'd rather walk to the south side.

Down to the river through a desert of car-parks and one-way signs, over the bridge. Which bridge? He stood against the ornate wrought-iron parapet to get his bearings, looking downriver to the railway line and upriver to the clustered trees of the Green, through the repeating struts of metal and concrete, a latticework of years. On a rock midstream a cormorant hung out its black wings to dry in the sun. Never saw that before. The river's different, it's clean. The city's cleaner than it used to be.

The Merchant City's cleaner. The old south side, it's just the same.

I'm just the same.

But he looked at the sleeve of his designer jacket, which was quite new. In daylight everything was different anyway. He still wasn't sure if this was the right bridge. A passing policeman gave him a sharpish look, one hand on the regulation radio, in case it might be necessary to call in. Some of the bridges were notorious for suicides, desperate people jumping over the side. Always had been. Matthew turned and strolled off the bridge, leaving the sun to dance on the skin of the glittering water, the hunting bird to dive into the thick depths below.

At first he thought it couldn't have been the right bridge. It led him into a strange new place with plazas, trees and grass, sculptures, sharp new apartment blocks. But beyond the clean bricks he saw the old sandstone of a church, and then a street-name he knew.

And he was in the long ancient street with its black tenements on either side, a canyon of desire. The crossroads, the clock and fountain. Shabby slouching men with their caps pulled low. Wifies in headscarves pushing ricketty prams. Matthew kept his head down, perusing their rusty hemlines, and soon enough got the flicker of long legs, a tall young blonde girl hurrying among the beaten-down mothers and grans. Never going to be like them.

'That's a disgrace so it is!' the wifies hissed at her heels. 'Skirt up to there! You can see her bloody bum!'

Matthew followed the long street round. It was Saturday night.

There was the dance-hall, the Moon and Stars, with the painted zodiac arching above its door where the dancers crowded in. Your fortune in the stars. Never going to be a wifie in a headscarf: she showed it in the pert switching of her mini-dress, the swagger of her long boots. She paid her money and went blithely in, ready for anything, and so did he.

One, two, three.

Saturday night? But it can't be, because Louise has gone to work. Matthew stood in the daylight street, opposite the shuttered disco, shaking something out of his head. A passing wifie gave him a hard stare. He marched off like somebody on important business, following the grid, since you couldn't go wrong that way.

Here and there something had happened to the grid, and again he found himself on sleek paved pedestrianised roads. But they still led to the bridge. He stood on the bridge, looking back to the old south side where it festered and swarmed. Behind him stretched the cool courts of the Merchant City. He turned round and sauntered home.

He found he was too warm before he got there, because he'd put his jacket on again, pulling the sleeves down to cover his shirt-cuffs. Silly! No need for that! He took his jacket off and strolled on, taking as long as he possibly could. In spite of that he was home in time for the early evening news.

Not much more than the paper had revealed, though they did have a picture of the latest victim. An old photograph, evidently, before she had cut her hair. Her mother was wheeled out to make an emotional plea, also a tear-stained friend, ugly as sin. Even flanked by policemen, the plain mousy thing was afraid. It was always the ugly ones who felt most at risk, for some reason Matthew couldn't explain.

'Sharon phoned me,' she whimpered. 'Ten days ago? Fortnight? She'd ben walking home and somebody had been following her, she said.' You could hear security doors slam, keys turn, chains slide and click, all over the south side.

A street-map filled the screen. The two major roads on the south side. The Moon and Stars; no, what's its name now? STREETS OF FEAR the caption cried, a bit alarmist in Matthew's view. Two locations, two dates, close together, determined as always to hype it up, never mind the facts. You saw the graphics and ignored the voice-over, which did have a more sober view of things. 'A man is in custody in connection with the first murder,' the presenter intoned, 'and police do not think the two incidents are linked.'

Margaret stood beside the television screen. Still she didn't speak. He wanted to ask her, but he never had. 'You are looking after me, aren't you?' he begged instead.

Louise's key in the door. An answer, he supposed.

9

He went out into the hall to meet her, and Margaret came too. Louise staggered into the kitchen under a great load of food and drink. Garlic bread. Double cream. Red wine. 'Oh, I say,' he said. 'Looking after me or what?'

'I didn't bother with lunch.' Louise unloaded goodies on to the table. 'Did something I never did before. Skipped lunch and just sat in the Square. Thinking about things.' She carried potatoes to the sink. 'So how was your day?'

'Oh, much the same as usual. Bit boring.' He started to tell her about it., but he couldn't seem to get it clear in his head. Her canvas shopper, stuffed with everyday odds and ends, slumped on the floor against a chair-leg. The corner of an evening paper stuck out. 'Shall I unpack this?' he suggested.

'No, leave it, I don't need that stuff yet. Must get these potatoes on.' It was taking longer than she expected. First one and then another, as she deftly peeled them, revealed ominous black bruises, and when she cut through the centre she found rot and decay. 'Bugger,' she said. 'This sometimes happens. I thought these were okay. To look at they're perfectly fine.'

He stared sickly at the smooth-skinned potatoes, each one rotten to the core.

At last she had found enough clean potatoes for a meal and they were bubbling on the stove. She took a moment to clear out her shopping-bag. Out came her scarf and gloves, not required on this sunny day, and she tossed them on a chair. Out came a box of tissues, discarded on to the floor. Out came the paper, a later edition than his, Matthew thought. He held his breath, but she skimmed the wad of pages carelessly across the room. It nearly hit Margaret, but she was insubstantial, a ghost. Couldn't be hurt any more.

'Louise,' he said, 'there's something I want to ask you.'

'Yeah, sure, darling, fire ahead.'

But she wasn't attending. She had tipped a load of vegetables on to the chopping-board and her quick hands were at work. Slicing, dicing, now the oil, the frying-pan. 'Where's the big wooden spoon?' she said.

'Is that all you're interested in?' he screamed.

She stopped dead, open-mouthed, her rummaging hands arrested in the kitchen drawer. 'I didn't –' she said. 'I never meant –'

Matthew saw that she hadn't meant anything of the kind. 'Sorry.' He grabbed her for a lifesaving hug.

'Louise,' he said into her flyaway hair. 'I've got to ask you. Won't you give up work and look after me?'

She was absolutely still in his arms. 'Stay at home? Like Margaret?' she said.

'Everything was all right,' he said, 'when Margaret looked after me.'

'I'm used to working, Matthew. You know? Wives do work nowadays?' She kept her head down so that he couldn't see her face. 'Margaret told me, but - '

'Margaret told you what, you stupid bitch?' he said.

But he couldn't have said it aloud, because she was wittering on. 'I thought it would be enough if we – If I – You know –'

A maiden glance below her eyelashes. The old shy virginal Louise. As if the alley had never seen what it had seen.

'Like Margaret,' he said. Shouldn't have said that. Perhaps he hadn't, because Louise didn't seem to have heard.

'But maybe that isn't enough.' She looked up at him now, a straight gaze that nevertheless he couldn't plumb. 'You said things worry you. Things happen that worry you.' For a moment he seemed to know what she was talking about, but she veered away again. 'No, I can see this, our marriage could be in trouble. I'll have to think about it.'

'You might stop work?' he begged.

'I think I might have to,' she said.

It was enough. He saw the calm days ahead. Safety with Louise in the quiet Merchant City squares. 'If you could,' he said, 'if you only could. I'm here on my own all day and – It's really important, Louise.'

'I know. I understand,' she soothed. As if perhaps she did. But she was speaking again and he knew in a rage that she didn't understand at all. 'There's just one thing.'

'What?' he barked.

'I tried to change it today.' She was very nervous. Frightened, you'd almost say. 'After I'd thought round it, you know? In the Square? Tried sounding out Gareth but it wasn't going to work.' Matthew knew he was staring at her. She had backed up against the freezer, nearly as white as its bland façade. 'Meant to tell you before now. Did mean to. Honestly. Only there's this weekend conference, you see, and I have to go.'

'A whole weekend?' he said, biting off each word.

'Friday to Sunday,' she said, 'yes.'

'What weekend, may I enquire?'

All in a rush: 'This weekend. Starting tomorrow in fact.' And a hopeful silly smile in case it wasn't really as bad as all that.

He left her in no doubt just how bad it was. When he had finished with her, corporate woman was no more. All my own work, he thought, with a kind of weary satisfaction. 'Friday to Sunday,' he repeated in measured tones. He had flayed her already and just those three words made her wince again.

'But I'll go as late as I can,' she offered in desperate hope. 'Our presentation's first thing Saturday but I won't leave here till late on Friday night. I'll make supper before I go, okay? And we've all got to socialise on Saturday night, but I'll come back on Sunday morning. In time for lunch, how about that?'

'If it's the best you can do.'

'You'll only be on your own for two nights. Thirty-six hours?'

'That's not the problem.'

But was it? He got up. It wasn't possible to stay still.

'Where are you going, Matthew?' she cried.

'I've got to think this over. I'm going out.'

'Where?'

'I don't know. The pub,' he said at random.

'You never go to the pub!'

'If you want to live your own life,' he said, 'then I can too.'

It sounded good, hanging in the air as he banged out of the door. In the lift he did realise that she had been twittering something or other as he stamped out. Forget the conference, maybe? I'll look after you, Matthew? He hesitated in the foyer, wondering whether to go back.

But he would seriously lose Brownie points if she found out he hadn't heard what she said. Weren't you listening? Don't you ever listen to me? Well, no, Louise, you see –

Can't explain really. He went out into the chill Merchant City evening. What I heard, Louise, what I was listening to –

Long-ago conversations. Old voices in his mind.

10

True enough, he never went to the pub. Hadn't for years. He hardly drank and Margaret never touched the stuff. How long since he had been in a pub on his own? On the doorstep of the steamy south-side local he stood aside politely to let a girl go ahead. Tall girl, mini-dress, long legs in kinky boots. She murmured thanks as she stepped inside.

When he got in he couldn't see her. It was as if she'd never been there at all.

He looked for a pound note to buy a drink with, but he didn't seem to have one. Banknotes were being brandished at the bar, but they weren't the small green things they ought to be. Could they be tens? Those couldn't be twenties surely? The gantry was full of names he didn't know. Strange drinks changed hands. The guy ahead of him ordered a Guinness, and that appeared to be much the same as it used to be. Matthew repeated the order and followed the guy in clapping down a largish note. He got a handful of change and for a moment he didn't recognise the coins. As on the night of full moon. He pushed that thought away.

He found a corner seat, back to the wall, and sat down, uncomfortable, out of place. Louise's fault. He should be sitting at home with Louise. The cosy picture of the two of them, side by side on the sofa, made his eyes sting with tears. There he'd be safe, he knew. Through the smoke, across the pub, he saw the tall girl again. Couldn't see her kinky boots, but in the dim air her blonde hair shone.

On his right and his left there was only one thing being talked about. Understandable, here on the south side, a hundred yards from the Moon and Stars.

'Well it's no the boyfriend this time, he's banged up,' said one guy, breathing a casually perfect smoke-ring above the heads of his pals. You could see how they would frequently feel like thumping him, and they rushed to correct him now.

'He never done the first yin. It's the same bastard whacked them baith.'

'He fuckin confessed to the first yin.'

'Confessed! That'll be shining!' several voices said.

Matthew, like a foreign tourist, translated the rhyming slang: that'll be shining bright, that'll be right. Pleased with himself, he missed the next few sentences, though police brutality seemed to be the theme.

'Naw, it's the same bastard, they've went and let him dae it again.'

'Naw, it's a copycat,' drawled the smoke-ring merchant.

'Naw, it's different,' said the seedy wee guy in the anorak on the edge of the group, who'd been hanging on every word, his eyes flicking like silverfish from face to face.

They looked at him. He kept them waiting. Lapping his half-pint, glancing aside, glancing up, he reeled them in. 'The second yin's different fae the first. The second yin was raped wi an instrument,' he said. 'So I heard.'

Matthew considered the expressions along the line. They didn't like that. The thought of an instrument. Not nice. And the thought of how the seedy wee guy might know. Not nice at all.

'Instrument? A saxophone dae you mean?' said some really sad joker. 'A Lambeg drum?' It died in the tight-drawn air.

'An instrument,' somebody else ventured to say. 'That wasny in the paper.'

'Naw, that could be evidence, see,' said the seedy wee man. 'They wouldny be allowed to print that.' For the first time in his whole life, maybe, people were listening to him. A half and a half-pint had appeared at his hand. 'I heard it from a guy. Nae idea where he heard it.' He licked up his drink in the consciousness of a job well done.

They were still trying to work it out. 'He found her maybe. The guy that telt you.'

'Or the guy that telt him, he found her.' Further than that they weren't prepared to go. Around the seedy wee guy, in the jam-packed pub, there was plenty of space. An exclusion zone.

That made the rest of the pub even more crowded. Matthew saw the tall girl fighting her way to the bar. 'Silly cunts, they're no here. They've went tae the wrang pub,' she was explaining to people as she passed, not that she knew them any more than she knew Matthew. She caught him looking at her and gave a half-grin, acknowledging that she was effectively talking to herself. To the barman, once she'd made it to the bar, she called 'See if two lassies come in? Lookin for me? Tell them I'm lookin for them in the Duck. I'll gie them hauf an hour.' And she was off, stalking on her kinky long legs past the discussion group.

They were still at it. 'Nae DNA,' somebody had realised. 'Everybody kens aboot DNA. That's how he done it wi an instrument. So they couldny get his DNA.'

'Or it could be a wumman,' said the copycat man. A *Taggart* fan, Matthew would hazard a guess, though he would never let on.

The saxophone man couldn't be kept down. 'Or a guy wi nae prick!' he cried in mock excitement. Probably mock. Nobody liked that at all.

Time to go.

Beyond the spilled light of the pub it was very dark. A sick old moon, nearly gone. Matthew tripped over something that rang and clattered against the kerb. A short length of narrow-bore piping. He picked it up, meaning to throw it in a bin. Certainly he didn't have it when he got home.

'Look at the time!' Louise cried. He did, and yes, it was a whole lot later than it ought to be. 'Where have you been?' she was yelling.

'You sound like my mother.'

'Sorry,' she said in a sulk.

She took his coat and he went into the living-room. Margaret was standing by the window, as he had found her now and again. Looking for him. 'Where have you been, Matthew?' she used to say. Quietly, not yelling like Louise.

She didn't ask this time, but then of course she didn't need to. 'You know, Margaret,' he said. 'You always knew.'

She was going to speak at last. Her lips parted and moved, grey and cracked as they'd been before she died. 'Knew what, Matthew?' she said.

Or he had made her say it. No, she had spoken all right. He could see the words spelled out in the air, like the smoke-rings in the pub.

Louise had fixed drinks and turned the lights low. She sat beside him on the sofa, still slightly nervous, he could tell. Because he had banged out of the house in a temper? Or not because of that? 'You'll have to be extra careful, Louise,' he said. 'There's been another girl murdered on the south side.'

'Yes, I know.'

The shock ran through him, blood and muscle and nerve. He thought she must feel it as they sat together, touching at elbow and thigh. But she was nodding at the evening paper. Last night's girl, Sharon, with the short hairstyle and the boot-faced friend. 'I read all about it. But I never go to the south side,' she said.

'That's true. And it always happens on the south side.'

'So far,' she agreed vaguely, reaching over to top up her glass, not really hearing what she was saying.

He heard. The quiet clean Merchant City streets fell away at his feet. Screaming darkness. It can't happen here.

He made himself answer, and talking helped. 'Oh, I reckon he comes from the south side. Or she.' Of course Louise didn't follow that. 'Heard some guys talking in the pub. They thought it could be a woman. Because of – Never mind.'

A silence. It had to break.

'This is worrying you, Matthew,' she said.

He sighed. He took the time to find the right words for what he wanted to say.

'I went out,' he said, 'because I needed to think this through. There's something I should have told you, Louise. Never told anyone this before.'

Never needed to, because Margaret knew.

'Once, long ago,' he said, in the diction of a fairy-tale, 'I did something very bad. Margaret got to know about it but she loved me all the same. She realised it had been a terrible mistake. She looked after me so that it would never happen again.'

And Louise should have said 'Something bad? What d'you mean?'

She didn't, though.

'Tell me more,' she whispered instead.

'I can't.'

'It's to do with murder,' her quiet voice said. For a dizzy moment he thought she did understand.

But she was going on: 'Whenever there's a murder, you get upset. Nothing unusual in that, Matthew, love. I know. I've read about it.'

The bookshelves in her bedsit; Matthew saw them now. The dusty patches and the clean patches, where she had very recently taken books off the shelves. That was the odd thing he'd been trying to recall. 'What have you read? Psychology, do you mean? True crime?'

'Oh, this and that. But now you've told me,' she said, 'everything's all right.' She was pressing against him, fiercely sweet. The oddity from the bedsit again. No, no, the oddity was the books, we've covered that. She took them off the shelves before I could see them. Nothing really odd there. Odd kind of books for a girl to read. That's what I might have thought. Nothing more.

Apple-blossom scent from her yearning body. She was ready and eager, but was he? He made a final effort, tired as he was. He raised his head and drew a finger down her cheek.

'I made a mistake,' he said, very low, 'and somebody died. I can't tell you any more. You wouldn't love me and I need you to love me. I need you, Louise.'

'And I need you.' She said no more.

Gentle seemed right for him at this time. Louise was a bit puzzled, a bit disappointed perhaps, but his stroking and caressing pleased her, and worked for him in the end. 'I'll look after you,' she was promising when they drew apart. 'Always, always.'

Matthew was floating irresistibly into sleep, away from the difficult, knife-edge, finally coped-with day. 'We'll have to see what happens,' he said.

They lay together as decorously as in the first days of their marriage; as decorous as he and Margaret had always been.

11

Seven o'clock in the morning. He knew the time, because Margaret was getting up. He felt her weight leave the mattress. A moment's dip as she sat on the edge to pull her stockings on. He opened his eyes a crack and saw her quick quiet movements, the old jersey pulled over her head, the working skirt.

The dreams of the night slipped away. Sometimes they left him looking at worse things ahead. But everything was all right, because Margaret was there.

'You knew but it didn't matter,' he murmured, half asleep.

'Knew what?' he heard her say.

No, that's right. There was nothing for her to know. He heard her downstairs, clinking milk-bottles, rattling the damper of the Aga, maintaining his safe world.

Louise turned and murmured in her sleep with a delicate snort and a sigh.

The sky through the window was wrong. No trees. A Merchant City eyrie, high above the trees, if there had been any trees. Matthew propped himself on an elbow and looked down at her drowsing face, softened and relaxed.

'Louise,' he said, 'it's gone seven o'clock.'

'Hmm. Go away.'

'It's Friday, you know. It's a working day.'

'No. Conference. Don't have to.' She drifted away again.

And he remembered, because in truth she had told him, that she wasn't expected in the office today. The weekend conference was deemed to have begun. Apparently that entitled her to sleep all day. He felt irritation build.

And a kind of fear.

I could have got up hours ago, he thought. I could be out of the house. Doing anything at all. She wouldn't know or care.

I could do anything. She wouldn't know.

'Matthew!' she screamed. 'Bloody hell!'

He had gone too far to stop. He shuddered in the joy of release. But she pulled away, scrambling up the bed. For some reason she was seriously discomposed. 'For God's sake, Matthew!' she yelled.

'What's the matter? You said I could.'

'I did not!'

'Maybe you were dreaming.' To make a joke of it was probably best. 'So what were you dreaming about, Louise, hey?'

'None of your bloody business.'

But at least it had got her up and she moved about the flat, putting the muesli packet on the table, setting coffee to bubble. Still a bit sulky, as if what he'd done wasn't just what husbands do. Sulky and somehow bored, as if she didn't want to be at home.

'It'll be lovely having you here all day.' He nearly added 'Like Margaret,' but thought perhaps he'd better not.

'Hmm?' As if she'd forgotten what they had arranged.

'You're not going till late. After supper. You said.'

She was playing with her muesli. 'The *point* of this day off,' she said, 'is to let me pack in the morning. Drive up at lunchtime. Have all afternoon at the conference. Network. You know.'

'Oh, network! Corporate woman!' he jibed.

'Yes! That's the idea!' She stared at him with her jaw set, as if they hadn't settled all of this before. 'You know, Matthew,' she said, trying to apologise, 'that's what I do best.'

He stood behind her, nuzzling her knotted-up hair. 'You don't know that,' he said, 'till you've tried doing other things.'

'Like looking after you?'

'There's no end to what you can do, Louise.'

'Right,' she said into her muesli. 'If I have the time and space.'

He stared down at her untidy head that bobbed slightly as she chewed. What did she mean? Margaret never talked like that. 'When you leave work you'll have all the time in the world.' Something wholly unlikely, something overheard, tugged at the back of his mind. Impossible. Well, not completely impossible. Unlikely. That's all.

'Anyway I'm going to have a bath,' she said, getting up. 'Since I've got all day. Lots of bubbles and steam.' As she rummaged for towels in the airing-cupboard he thought she said 'Good place to think,' but he could have misheard. When she emerged with her fluffy armful she was only saying 'I may be some time.'

'Don't be too long. I've got nothing to do. I love it when you're here.'

For a moment, in the haze of the steamy bathroom, he thought she was going to cry. 'Oh, Matthew.' She came close and stroked his cheek. 'If I'm at home - ' she said, and seemed to search for words to make it clear. 'If I do stop work, it'll have to be a different shape of day. We'll have to talk. Not now, eh?'

She disappeared into the scented steam. Over her shoulder she called 'Why don't you go out for a walk? Lovely day.'

'I could get a paper,' he said.

'Sure. And a sandwich for lunch, yeah? Prawn cocktail for me.'

He waited for a bit, because the dailies would have gone to press too soon. When he was pretty sure the first edition of the evening paper would be on the stands, he walked briskly in the bright morning, enjoying the spring sun, enjoying even the feel of the smooth clean paving-slabs under his feet. It's good to be here, he thought. It was an echo from two weeks ago but why shouldn't it still be true? A new city, a new beginning. I'm learning to make decisions and I make them well.

He picked up a paper, sorting out the right change. The newsvendor nodded grumpily. For a moment Matthew thought that was bad. But the next guy tried to offer a tenner, and that's what the vendor would recall about this day.

Early though it was, the evening paper had the overnight news. CITY's NIGHT OF MURDER, the hysterical headline screamed. Matthew walked back, reading, and shouldered distractedly through the revolving door, holding the paper open at the full stretch of his arms. A quite different city came out of the smudged pages. Sordid, scary, old.

NIGHT OF MURDER. What did that amount to then? A stabbing in one of the sad north-eastern housing schemes. A scuffle in the city centre, one dead. A girl murdered on the south side, near a popular local pub, the White Swan, commonly known as the Duck. Not many details, since her body had only just been found when this edition went to press. It did seem as if everything had happened at much the same time: CITY's TEN MINUTES OF MURDER, the sub could have chosen to put instead.

But they were hyping the terror again. Matthew had seen the technique so often before. If they said TEN MINUTES, then you wouldn't see so clearly what you were being teased to see. One killer responsible for it all. One black figure, shapeless and faceless, moving north to south through one long night across the shrinking city's streets.

The lift was in transit, heading for the upper floors. He thought of taking the stairs, but he didn't quite feel up to it: nothing serious, a catch in the breath, a slight trembling in the legs. Too much coffee, must watch out for that. On the thought came a warm safe feeling that he couldn't account for just at first, but in a moment he realised why. Soon Louise would be at home all day, anxiously replacing the coffee, if she thought it advisable, with decaff or camomile tea. Looking after him. Soon.

The lift had stopped to collect someone on its way down. Here in the Merchant City, as Louise and he had long agreed, you didn't meet your neighbours, but wouldn't you know they'd put in an appearance when you wanted to use the lift? Matthew waited as patiently as he could, using the time to read the paper with care. In the flat it wouldn't be convenient to go over and over the story under Louise's sharp eyes.

The lift doors slid open and the tall blonde girl from the office party stepped out. Keys in her fingers, still shrugging on her jacket, since she had just stepped out of her flat.

They'd been neighbours all along.

Automatically he got into the lift. It was cold, as if the sides were open to the plunging shaft. As he stepped out on his own landing he realised he'd forgotten to get the fucking sandwiches. He jumped back in before the doors closed and rode right down again. The girl was in the residents' car-park, flipping her keys to unlock a sporty little car.

She gave a finger-fluttering wave to a window high above. The morose partner. They'd been at the party together, they came out together, grabbing a taxi while Matthew and Louise had to walk home. He saw a split-screen image of what must have happened then. Matthew and Louise at ground level, down and dirty, thrusting and gasping in the alley mud. High in the block of flats, the blonde girl and her man. Crisp sheets under a trendy pine headboard, but down and dirty, just the same.

Where was their flat? Above? Left or right? Next door or two flats away?

He thought it was just underneath his flat. Louise sprawled beneath him, creamy billows, secret darkness there and there and there. On the floor below, so near, he saw the blonde girl, the long slim legs outstraddled, all gold.

'Prawn cocktail and *what* did you say?' the guy in the delicatessen snarled. He got back to the flats somehow and rode up in the lift once more, seeing nothing of what was there.

Maybe she doesn't live here. Been here for an overnighter, dirty little cat. Needn't ever see her again.

But he knew that wasn't so.

Should have checked the names on the entryphone. Don't know her name. Don't need to. His key stuttered in the lock.

'Louise!' he called in the hall. It's going to be all right. Louise is here. Like Margaret. To look after me.

Louise came out of the bedroom and she was in her conference clothes, smart and groomed and ready to go. 'Look, it's silly,' she was saying. Nervous behind the bright façade. 'Staying here all day with nothing to do? And you see, love, they're really expecting me this afternoon. I'm going to have a sandwich and get on the road.'

'You said you'd make my supper.'

'Oh that's all right! Sorted!' Proudly she led him to the fridge and exhibited a beautifully dressed salad, ready on its plate, dewy under clingfilm. Tiny pork pies to go with it. An individual trifle. A jug of cream.

Not the work of ten minutes. Something very wrong here.

'You prepared that ahead of time,' he said. 'You always meant to go.'

Or maybe he didn't say it. It echoed, though, in the clear Merchant City air. Nothing can happen here.

Louise, you mustn't go, because -

No. No.

Munching her prawn cocktail on wholemeal, she reached across for the paper. He waited on a precipice of fear, though he hardly knew why. She flipped through the pages and back to the screaming headline. She spent some time on the city's NIGHT OF MURDER, moving from crime to crime.

And back again. The stabbing, the scuffle, the south-side murder. Louise hadn't taken particular notice of the south-side murder, any more than the paper had. The girl from the pub was only a leaf in the forest of the city's night of crime.

That would change very soon, he knew.

Louise raised big worried eyes. 'Does all this bring it back to you, Matthew?' she said.

He couldn't answer, couldn't move.

'Though it's so long ago,' she said. 'Thirty years and more?' She was gazing at him now, all pity and understanding. 'What you told me. When someone died.'

He swallowed and couldn't reply. Beside him on the sofa, all among the teacups and sandwich crumbs, she was at his zip, and she'd moved his hand to correspond.

'What I think - ' Apparently she didn't mind disarraying her conference clothes. The jacket slipped off, the white shirt opened hole by hole. 'When you lived with your mum it must have been difficult for you.' Butterfly kisses on his mouth and a pussycat smile as her fingers reached their goal. 'And somebody died. But then you married Margaret and you were happy. She looked after you. And now it's my job.'

'You look after me,' he said. 'You do everything that Margaret did for me.'

'And more, I bet,' she said, muffled. 'And more.'

'You keep me safe.' Safe in a new life. In the Merchant City death couldn't come. He gripped her in blinding fear.

'I keep you safe,' she was trying to say. 'I give you what you need.'

Which seemed to be what she needed too. 'Is this too rough for you?' he gasped.

'You're never too rough for me.' The lamp behind his head reflected in her eye, a single star. 'You were never too rough with Margaret, were you?'

'No. I was never angry with Margaret.' Hardly ever. 'I'll never be angry with you.'

'You don't have to be. This is what to think about. And this. And this.' Too much? She was loving it all. 'Matthew,' she gasped, 'I will leave my job. It'll be worth it.' He hadn't time to wonder what exactly she might mean.

'Oh Matthew. Oh yes. Oh yes. Oh yes. One. Two. Three.'

He couldn't stop. Black lightning. He lay on top of her, exhausted. She couldn't have said what he had heard her say.

'Oh God! Look at the time!' She rolled off the sofa and away. In and out of the shower, bundling her crumpled, stained clothes into the laundry-basket, into the built-in wardrobe for a fresh pressed jacket and skirt, a blouse so white it dazzled the eye. Hair, mascara, blusher, while he sat drained on the sofa with his hands between his thighs. She hopped in the doorway, putting on her shoes, tossing car keys and flat keys from hand to hand.

'Two nights, that's all. You'll hardly notice I'm gone. Back for Sunday lunch.' She blew kisses across the room, to which he couldn't respond. 'And then I'll look after you. You'll never need to think about it again.'

Something very wrong.

She waved and went out, a woman he used to think he knew. What turns her on?

Violence turns her on. Death turns her on.

No. Still not quite right. Scrupulous as a poet, he sought the exactly right word. Killing turns her on.

He pushed that thought away, but it stayed to tempt him. Part of the thing that was very wrong. The short day was over and streetlights shone in the Merchant City outside. Matthew got up from his lengthy spell on the sofa, stiff as an old man. He turned on lamps and drew curtains. New curtains soon, planned by Louise. She has plans for the flat that she doesn't share with me. Plans for her life. She does things I don't know about. She's thirty-five years old and I haven't known her for as much as a year.

Margaret sat on the sofa writing a letter to Louise.

He flicked the TV remote, saw a grave-faced newsreader, thumbed the sight away.

Killing excites Louise. He thought about that.

Matthew picked up the evening paper again while the voices in the pub played over in his ear. Street-maps and graphics across the middle-page spread, like the diagrams in a classic detective story. Where the sleuth takes a big piece of paper, sets down the dates and the times and the facts, and the truth comes clear.

He found the pile of old newspapers, stacked up by Louise in a moment of briskness but never properly cleared away. Junk mail in the wastebasket yielded three or four sheets of A4 paper, blank on one side. He took them into the kitchen, spread them out on the table, found a biro, used the edge of Louise's shopping-list pad as a ruler, drew a series of straight lines, vertical and horizontal on the page. A grid, a chart, began to form under his hand. He felt he was about to discover something he didn't know. In the silence of the undefended flat he heard the lift whine again, carrying the blonde girl to her partner's bed.

12

With craftsmanlike care Matthew worked on his chart. He had ruled lines from top to bottom of his sheet of paper to give four columns, but on reflection he made that five. A horizontal line across the top. Above the columns he printed headings in block capitals. DATE, then TIME, then DETAILS OF MURDER. Essential, all three.

The next heading. How to put it? MOON/STARS/WEATHER, he wrote. He saw at once, in a lightning-flash, how that would help the investigation. Then the knowledge was gone as suddenly as it had come. But it was there, inside his head.

Now the fifth heading, the important one. Again he wasn't quite sure how to phrase it. Whereabouts? Alibi? But he saw it at last. All he needed to say: WHERE WAS LOUISE?

To fill in the details he went to the big stack of newspapers that Louise had kept. He found not just the evening papers she regularly brought home, but several dailies, tabloid and broadsheet both. She had bought them without telling him, read them, stacked them up in a corner of the room. Thinking he would never notice? He read them with great care now.

DATE. That was easy. Just a couple of days ago, and he confirmed that with the papers. Wednesday and Thursday back to back, which had pleased the journos no end. TIME. They'd got that accurately enough, give or take an hour or two. DETAILS OF MURDER. A lot to go in here. The locations, close together. On the south side, of course. The full names of the victims, which he hadn't known before. Didn't need to know.

'Louise didn't need to know,' he corrected himself, but nevertheless he wrote them down.

No mention of an instrument, but thanks to the wee guy in the pub that was no secret now. He wrote them down. A wooden spoon for the Wednesday murder. A length of narrow-bore piping on Thursday. Outside the pub in the stinking mud. DETAILS was getting rather crowded. Should have planned it better. In case there was more to come.

MOON/STARS/WEATHER. Nothing in the papers of course. Yet it was so clear, a necessary thing. He wrote down what he remembered. An old moon. An occasional star.

And the last column. He searched his memory and checked the calendar, and found no doubt at all. Wednesday, Louise at her launch, or supposed to be. Thursday, Louise alone in the flat. With a car at her disposal to take her across the bridge into the south side.

As an afterthought he found a red biro and starred some days, some times, when she had seemed unusually excited. That appeared to fit too. Killing turns her on.

He stared at the chart, satisfied. Louise killed them all.

He'd been writing for hours and he very much needed to go to the loo. He paused for a moment at the full-length mirror in the hall. For a moment it was Louise he saw in the glass, amoral and strange.

Of course it was his own reflection, red-eyed in the cold dawn light. He pulled away, went into the toilet, let the constricted water go at last, sighing in ease. When Louise saw herself in the mirror, what did she see? He stumbled into the bedroom and collapsed on the bed, shirt and trousers and all.

He woke in the clear spring Merchant City morning with gulls crying far away.

High clouds drifted across the window and he seemed to be drifting, directionless, too. As he had drifted in the misery of the funeral, before Louise came bustling in to take him in hand. With some difficulty he worked out that it was Saturday now. A strange, strange Saturday, with no Margaret, no Louise. An unstructured Saturday, with its shape yet to find.

The shape of Saturday. He'd never had to think about it before.

Saturday with Margaret. Structured, like every other day.

Again he felt the bed dip and swing as she got out. 'Half-past eight?' he murmured, ready for a modest lie-in.

'The shopping, dear,' she reminded him over her shoulder as she went down to poke up the Aga. He saw her clearly, jerseyed spine and stout tweed skirt, and the bedroom door with its graceful mouldings closing at her back. The flush-panelled pale-wood Merchant City door gleamed dimly behind all that, less real.

They walked briskly round the neighbourhood shops. He held the basket while she loaded the fresh good produce in. The neighbours were out too, south-side husbands and wives together, the way it used to be. No sign of the blonde daughter. She would be at home, stretched lazily, long bare limbs, in bed.

The couple on the other side bared their teeth at him in a ghastly grin, strawberry-faced from the killing car.

Then home for lunch. Potter in the garden, sheltered by the high hedges on every side. A casserole for dinner, which Margaret had slipped into the oven, he couldn't say when. Then television, tea and biscuit, bed. Hardly ever broken, the shape of Saturday, during his married life.

Broken, or altered. Changed back to an older shape? Drowsy in his bed, he thought that might be nearer, but the memory slipped away. Once or twice perhaps. Maybe three times.

'How often?' he heard Margaret say. But he couldn't have heard it. She didn't know.

She lay on the sofa with the TV remote to hand. 'It's all right. It's a back muscle, it'll pass. Shouldn't have lifted that tub on my own.' He brought her cups of tea. Soluble aspirin, plenty of it, to take the edge off the pain. 'Thank you, dear,' she said, and her heavy eyelids fell. He went out. She never knew.

He was sure she had never known.

He saw her by the window waiting and worrying for him to come home, her fingers teasing up and down the edge of the red velvet curtain, where there was a rubbed strip now.

In bed, this bed, with migraine. He stood beside her, because even his weight on the bed made it worse, she said. 'It's called the Saturday disease,' she murmured with a pale smile. 'Stress. It's stress easing up, really. End of the week, people come home.'

'Sleep it off, dear,' he said. 'It's the only cure.' He took the chance to go out. To leave her asleep.

A bit rushed, those Saturdays, because you didn't know when the migraine might lift, and of course he didn't have the option of the car. 'You never exactly *encouraged* me to drive, did you?' he said to the sleeping mound in the bed. He blinked in the sun that fingered through the curtains. Didn't *want* me to? He turned his head away.

He had managed to do what he wanted to, all the same.

'Worry can bring on cancer.' The desperate grip of her bird-boned hand.

'That's an old wives' tale,' he said aloud in the Merchant City morning sun. A wifie in a headscarf scuttled out through the shining bedroom door.

He got up, showered, shaved, threw his crumpled clothes into the laundry-basket. Saturday with Louise, now, was a much lazier day. She cooked from the freezer, and, having no garden, they didn't have to go outside at all. Hardly even got out of bed. But, he remembered, scraping toast-crusts into the bin, lazy wasn't exactly the word. That's why I'm drifting. I'm missing Louise.

He smashed the plate against the mixer tap, taking himself by surprise.
I will never be angry with Louise.

He cleaned up the sink, trapping porcelain shards safely with a damp cloth, the one domestic skill he had developed over the years. He ran cold water on a cut finger and found a plaster in the first-aid box he had insisted Louise should buy. The protective plastic flaps were awkward to peel off and he had to lick up a drop of blood that welled from the tiny wound.

No.

She ought to be here. If she was here - She ought to be here.

His chart was still spread out on the table in Louise's bleak sunny kitchen, the sad vinyl and formica pale as a dead face. He sat down to start on it again, but a headachey reluctance warned him he'd overdone things a bit. Arty-farty types said it on the telly: you couldn't hurry a work in progress. A work of art, no, a work of research, really. When it was finished, and it soon would be, something would be clear that he saw only in glimpses now. Through a glass darkly. He stared out at the clean morning Merchant City and saw the glittering Moon and Stars in the south-side night.

'We'll leave it to rest,' Margaret said, stepping back from the Aga with a satisfied nod. Of course it was the bread she was talking about, the creamy swelling loaves on the plate-rack. Couldn't be the chart. Because she didn't know.

He went out into the Saturday town.

In the entrance hall he paused to look up and down the entryphone panel, a stacked column of unfamiliar names. Hansen, one floor down? Could be. Though of course she wasn't necessarily an ethnic blonde. That always annoyed him a bit. Dark roots you could spot beforehand, but not the hidden deception, where it ought to sparkle gold and instead was mousy brown.

He got a flash of that picture of her again, sprawled in clean yuppie sheets with her bad-tempered man. He checked every angle and it was as he'd imagined. All gold. Blonde through and through.

Hansen. His finger hovered over the bell. It mightn't be her name. Don't have to know her name.

'Hello,' he said. The blonde daughter from next door gave him a dirty look. 'Don't be scared,' he said, 'we're neighbours, you know.'

'Fuck off, you creep.'

Scarlet to the ears, he stamped through the shining Merchant City, cannoning off the street furniture. People stopped and stared. He slowed his pace, tamed his breathing, paused to buy a paper, finding the right change with a genial remark for the woman behind the stall. Danger. Great danger. He'd got angry for no reason. Worked himself up into a rage over something which, let's face it, the little bitch probably never said. Language like that on the south side!

The odd thing, now the rage had gone, was how good he felt. As if something exciting was going to happen. And he was going to make it happen, the great exciting thing.

What he felt, he realised, was young.

This drenching cleansing kind of rage belonged with being young. But he'd always had to look over his shoulder guiltily for the punishment he knew would come. Before Louise, even before Margaret, his mother was there. Control yourself, Matthew! He couldn't, as she should have known. I'll give you something to cry about! And in the red madness of the punishment he lost all control. He didn't remember that at all well.

A little later he was taller than his mother. A bag of nerves she was, constantly on edge, but it was her fault of course. Their fault. She was helpless and she knew it. She hindered him all the same, just by being there.

He stopped at a crossing, alone in the shopping crowd. At last. Again. In the brief time between his mother and Margaret, he remembered from long ago, he had been able to get into a rage without guilt, with no punishment to fear. He had been alone.

And truly himself. He knew that for a moment, stranded on the pavement as the shoppers surged to and fro. The shape of those Saturdays. He remembered now.

Margaret trudged along at his elbow, more real than the sparkling town. 'You don't know about this,' he said to her. A young man on his way to the dancing. Black night around him and he saw the buzzing foyer of the Moon and Stars. A blonde girl laughing in the neon light. 'See you later,' she said to her pal. Though she wouldn't. He knew.

No, it was a daytime Saturday and he was walking west along a pedestrian precinct, girls in denims and Docs whisking by. Wifies shuffling on their old sore feet. The great department stores rose up beside him, the only places his mother ever shopped; he waited for her, arms full of parcels, in the clanging street outside. But she was gone, long gone. So were the stores. Trendy black-painted benches and litter-bins were strung out along the street, no, the precinct, it was called now. But a tramcar sailed past where no tramlines were. A galleon in the dark, heading for the south side.

He came to Charing Cross and saw a hotel on one corner and a tearoom on the other, full of supping wifies gossiping over their scones. A tearoom, was that right? The motorway and its bridges looped under and over the road and he couldn't quite remember what used to be there. Some things he didn't remember, they'd gone.

They could be recalled, though.

On the far side of the motorway the great green dome of the Mitchell Library, a giant brain, held them all. Matthew waited for the crossing signal, pleased with himself, pleased to find the purpose of the day. I'm not mad. That's why I came this way.

As Louise had told him, research was easy now. Janitors were checking briefcases and rucksacks, but Matthew had nothing suspicious about him and he walked straight in. A lift to level five, Louise had said, and you don't actually have to ask the staff. They didn't have to bring great bound files up to your desk. Sturdy little microfilm boxes were shelved round the walls, each box dated, month and year, and you took what you wanted yourself. He chose a year and picked out three boxes: November, January, March. Together they spanned a winter that he knew.

Watching the earnest woman at the next machine, he soon got the hang of threading up the microfilm. November first of all. The facts were there, most of them known to him. Of course there were some things he remembered which weren't in the paper, clear as they'd been at the time. The warm dance-hall welcome of the Moon and Stars. Black flames in the south-side sky. A single star.

January: he remembered that too. Further facts appeared, though some hadn't been printed which both papers and police quite certainly knew. From his detective stories Matthew was wise to that trick.

More interesting was March, a much longer report. By then, as he recalled, they'd compiled a spread of photographs and headlines. They had tied everything together and given the package a name. He came to the page he clearly remembered, the page which he had seen in black lightning above Louise's gasping head. The numbers across a double spread. One, two, three.

He tried the numbers out for the first time in thirty years, turning them silently in his mouth. In this city, even now, you wouldn't want to say them aloud. The three photographs. Three girls on the south side. Swaggering into the Moon and Stars, turning at the entrance, waving to friends they would never see again. All blonde girls. All Saturday nights.

Pleased with his prowess on the microfilm reader, he got a fourth box off the shelf. June. A wedding notice. Matthew John to Margaret Jane. Plain names. Plain people, living a quiet life in their big house. Husband and wife, a couple, just like the other couples on the respectable south side.

'This is so sudden, Matthew,' Margaret had said. No, she hadn't of course. In the early days he had occasionally teased her about her maidenly reluctance, and when he did he used that easily-laughed-at cliché.

What she had said was more pointed by far.

'But Matthew, it's all a bit quick, isn't it? Why are you asking me now? Any special reason why?'

'I couldn't ask you while my mother was alive,' he explained.

His mother had died six months ago. She didn't point that out. Accepting him, she accepted his reason for proposing that spring. Or so it seemed to him.

'Poor Matthew, you've had a hard time. I'll look after you,' she said.

He took down yet another box, the September of the previous year. His mother's death notice. Matthew read it with care, as he'd read it then. He felt, as then, the reflex of pain and humiliation, followed by the slow spreading joy.

He could do everything he wanted to do now.

He put the microfilm boxes away in their numbered slots and yielded his machine to a mad-looking man in a greasy mac, slavering to add details to a dirty dream.

The day had gone, though he didn't know where. He walked through the Merchant City, quiet in the dark of the moon. The glow of the streetlights fell short of the weathercock and above it there was a single star.

He knew the tall blonde girl would come. It was that sort of night. She was coming home to the flats hand-in-hand with her partner, but she stopped under the entrance light.

'Oh bugger,' she said. Language like that here! 'I meant to get milk. Look, you go on up, I can get some round in Candleriggs, won't be long.'

She turned and ran out of the courtyard, past Matthew, never looking his way. Fuck off, she might as well have said. The cleansing anger returned. He felt good, he felt young.

'Hello, Ms Hansen,' he said. Maybe that was her name after all, because she did turn round.

One blow to the head, yes, that's best, and she was easily enough hauled into the alley, where the old house poked its witch's-hat roof into the black sky. Off come the tights and that's easily done too. He had forgotten to pick up anything useful, but it didn't matter, because Louise was lying there with her skirts up, her moon-bleached hair, her big wide eyes. He plunged down on her in the smells of death and decay. The high buildings that lined the alley cut out the streetlights' glare, and when he'd finished he saw, like a seal of approval, the single star.

There was a lot of blood. Yes, there sometimes used to be. Blame the media, he thought; no, blame Louise, she put it into my mind; and he scrawled in blood on the shining cobbles the figures one, two, three.

The old shape of Saturday. As he'd always known. From the corner that led round into the clean new Merchant City he looked back at the alley. In the shifting moon-shadows he couldn't quite see her lying there.

13

Matthew got up and had a shower. Back in the bedroom he tidily smoothed the duvet over anything that might be there. He stood pondering whether something else had to be done. He had never used the washing-machine here, but when he went through into the kitchen it proved to be the same as the one in the south-side house. For the first time this flat felt like a safe place, his home.

He stuffed last night's clothes into the silvery drum, and added his sheet and duvet cover, just in case. In the big house the noise had never reached Margaret, drowsing her migraine away.

The chart, glimmering on the kitchen table, set things straight in his mind. Louise killed a girl last night.

He drew a line below the second murder and entered the third under yesterday's date. He jotted the details down quickly, because they were so clear still. He called the girl Ms Hansen, though he didn't know her name. Didn't need to know. In column four he noted that it had been the dark of the moon.

Column five still to fill in. He'd saved it till last, a bonne bouche. WHERE WAS LOUISE? Away at a conference (supposed to be).

And he was in the car with her, coming home. Apple-blossom scent: she was showered and shampooed, dressed from the clean skin out in fresh new clothes. The stuff she'd worn last night was in a plastic bag, knotted tight. She had run out early to stow it in her car, away from the chambermaid's eye. She stopped in a lay-by, unobserved on the quiet Sunday road, and flung the bulky soft bundle into a field behind the hedge. Cows prodded it with curious soft noses till the tight-stretched plastic burst. At the gust of blood they threw their heads up and galloped away.

Blood in the car. She'd have to get rid of it. He stood on the quayside and saw the little car, unbraked, roll forward, hesitate, nudge its blunt snout into empty space, tip in slo-mo over the edge. Turning boot over bonnet in the thick riverside air. Into the black water, down, down, washing away the blood, all stain of sin.

Greatly daring, he got another sheet of paper and plotted the details of the very first murder. The boyfriend in custody, but nothing proved. A fortnight before that Wednesday and Thursday on the dark south side. It all checked out once more, columns one to five, complete. Blood in the car.

No, hang on, there was stuff that Louise had to bring back from the conference: suitcases, briefcases, folders, bags. Walking through Sunday-morning streets with heavy cases would only draw attention to herself. She'd have to come home first. With the car. And the blood, and the sin.

He went to the window and looked out over the shining Merchant City, now full of police cars. A sort of caravan, which would be the incident room, he knew. Photographers and TV crews. Odd to think that with a few words he could clear it all away.

'Excuse me, inspector,' he'd say.

He went into the back room. In the clean streets of the Merchant City you got the reassuring official view. Down in the alley, in the mud and blood and graffiti, he saw what was really going on. He saw Ms Hansen, all gold. He saw Louise writhing under the moon. That's what it's like, the city sky. If a moon, no stars. If stars, no moon.

He remembered standing in the back court, long, long ago, the roar and the flame of Dixon's Blazes unheard, unseen behind the cliff of the tenement wall. They had come out to see the eclipse. Who on earth was standing behind him? Beside him was his mother, laughing, while the deep voice, behind them both, pointed out the strange things they should see. The moon was dead, copper-coloured, hanging in the sky. All round in dizzying glory, the stars.

'I'll give you something to cry about,' his mother said.

One, two, three.

And Margaret was there to save him, as always. 'Come on,' she said, 'I'm looking after you.' They went out through the foyer, which was packed with police. The fair-haired guy from *Taggart* was shepherding Ms Hansen's morose partner home from the morgue. The ugly face was a mask of tears. 'I'll give you something to cry about,' said a voice in Matthew's head.

In the sparkly city the pavements trembled like raspberry jelly, like his bare knees as he waited in his room. His mother's footsteps on the stairs. Margaret had disappeared, but there was Louise's little car, the only solid thing in the shaking street. He waved her down and she stopped. She stared at him, and her face went white under the corporate-woman shell.

He slipped in beside her. 'You can't go home,' he said.

A pause. Her voice, when she spoke, was hoarse as if she'd been crying. 'Why not, Matthew?'

'The police. They're everywhere.'

She looked over his shoulder and he turned to follow her gaze. He saw the police, and among them, walking with beautiful confidence by the side of her ugly man, a long-legged blonde ghost. Who couldn't be there. 'Reverse here,' he said to Louise. 'High Street will do.'

'Where are we going?' she croaked.

He hadn't known until that moment, but of course it had to be. 'To the south side.'

She made a terrible clumsy gear-change with a grating, crashing noise. 'You haven't been drinking, I hope?' Matthew teased.

She didn't reply. He saw that the radio was tuned to the local station. She'd been listening to the details of the murders. One, two, three.

'Did you stop and wipe the blood off the seats?' he enquired as they waited at a red light.

She slid him a white-eyed look. She must be very, very frightened indeed. For a moment he almost felt sorry for Louise.

14

They drove across the bridge. Dirty river, rimmed with close high buildings on either side. Two bridges downstream a southbound locomotive, picking up speed, jetted out its stately plumes of steam. They came to the crossroads with its fountain, the idling men, the shawled wifies hurrying by.

'This is where it was, Louise,' Matthew said.

'Yes.' As if she knew. How could she know?

He indicated with a finger the road she should follow, where the oil-stained flames from the high stalks cut the heavy air, and then the next street along. But she passed its dark mouth and didn't turn until the second on the left.

'I said that one!' he yelled.

'That was one-way.' A shake in her voice, no wonder. He knew there were no one-way streets on the south side.

She made another left turn and seemed to think they were back on course. Scraps of police tape fluttered blue and white at the edge of a makeshift car-park. A development site. That wasn't right. He blinked and got the scene back as it ought to be, the clustered crumbling houses black with years. Wifies in shawls and slippers scuttered like beetles on the edge of sight.

'That's it,' he said. 'There's the dance-hall. The Moon and Stars.'

'The what?'

'Just here, look!'

She still couldn't seem to see it. 'The disco, do you mean?'

The painted zodiac, the garish neon sign, slipped to and fro. He directed Louise to park on a stretch of wasteground, a bare place with no memories, no threats. As it seemed to be. Really it was Dixon's Blazes where black flames roared to the sky. 'It was just here. This is the locus,' he explained, 'that's what they call it in detective stories. This is where it happened.'

'Those murders. Those girls.'

'Yes, those girls,' he said impatiently. 'And the One Two Three murders too.'

'You don't have to tell me, Matthew,' Louise said. 'I know.'

He blinked at her. Terribly frightened but determined, she stared back at him. 'I've read it up,' she added in a sort of apologetic way.

Read it up. *Studied* it. Microfilm spools reeled in his brain through years and streets and girls. But he saw the ghosts of books on her bedsit shelves. She read about it and hid the books from me.

Dusty shelves. The dust of months, maybe years. Long before our first date, before we ever met, she was reading about me.

She had turned in the driver's seat to face him, one hand draped over the wheel. 'You were the One Two Three killer,' she said. Margaret had never said those words.

Louise wasn't Margaret, though. Louise was different. He blinked into her bright wide-open excited eyes. Oddly different, oddly excited, was Louise.

'You told me you did something bad,' she said, 'once. One bad thing. You told me it was a terrible mistake, but that wasn't true, Matthew. You were the One Two Three killer and you killed three girls.'

One Two Three! They wouldn't let it go!

They were touching and he felt the thrill of tension through clothes and skin. She was very, very frightened. Excited, too.

'But you married Margaret,' she said, 'and settled down. And you were safe for all those years. Because Margaret loved you. Even though she knew.'

Margaret stood before him in her sixties gear. No, never that, with its little short skirts and kinky boots. A flowered cotton frock and a cardigan. 'This is so sudden, Matthew,' she said.

'Maybe not from the start,' Louise was saying. 'Maybe she suspected.'

'A bit quick, Matthew. Any special reason why?' Margaret said with her big calm eyes.

'But after a while she did know. You must surely have known that she knew.'

You're not going out? By yourself?

If you ever do that again, Matthew, I think you know what I'll do.

'Then she got ill. She was worried –' Louise hesitated, and over her voice he heard Margaret's voice again.

'Matthew, what's going to happen now?'

Still the same old frock and cardigan, though she lay exhausted on her sofa after the treatment that did no good. The doctor, the consultant, the rosy-faced minister trooped by. He had brought them to her, knowing they didn't have the answer. He didn't have the answer himself. What's going to happen now?

'She wrote to me about it,' Louise was saying in the steamy car.

The letters. Which had disappeared. Louise had caused them to disappear.

'You knew,' he said, 'when you married me.'

Hello, Matthew, I'm Margaret's friend.

'She knew that if she looked after you,' Louise said, 'you wouldn't do it again. I've tried to look after you like Margaret. Who would look after you if you – if I wasn't here?'

She leaned forward, unzipping, stroking him. Terrified. He could feel that. But it was the oddness of her that filled the car. Terrifying, too.

'I just want to tell you,' she said, 'that it doesn't matter to me.'

Killing turns her on.

It's worth it, she had said, long ago, or what seemed like long ago. Her hands and mouth were at work, his mouth on her bare body, where she wanted it to be. He felt his power rise and he knew she felt it too. He knew it could go too far. She knew it. That's what turns her on. The glamour of evil. That's what it's always been. He couldn't stop and she counted out loud, triumphant. Margaret lay docile beneath him as he thrust. One, two, three. Four, five, six. And on.

Back to the south side, the other south side, leaving the tree-shaded avenues and gracious houses behind. Back to the mean streets around the Moon and Stars, where it all began. He was there, it was happening, he was young. The smoky flames of Dixon's Blazes and above them a single star. A girl going into the Moon and Stars to look for a man. Her fault. The mini-dresses, the tights and the little silky knickers. Nobody knew about DNA then.

Another girl waving goodbye to her pal in the foyer. Another girl, or the same one, now he wasn't sure. So many blonde girls, and flickering memories of more. So many, in those few months of freedom, his mother safely dead.

What she did to me. Vivid as ever in the shrinking flesh. What I wanted to do.

Louise was a happy bride, tidying herself up after what husbands and wives do. 'As long as somebody looks after you,' she said. 'First Margaret, now me.'

'No. First my mother,' he said.

She stood before him in her graveclothes; no, in the crossover apron that swathed her from neck to knee. He had only been looking. It was them, the girls; they'd taken off their wet swimsuits, laughing in the sunny back green. Their fault. She dragged him inside, upstairs, and he was crying already because he'd had it before. 'I'll give you something to cry about,' she said. He tried to punch her but she held him across the bed. And she took his pants down. Their fault. Not mine.

Or her fault. Has to be. Or Margaret's, those bloody migraines. Louise's fault now. He remembered something he had totally forgotten, the reason he had brought Louise to the south side.

'No, you've got it completely wrong, Louise,' he said. 'I'll tell you how it was. You killed them all.'

15

He made her start the car and take him round the murder sites once more. Her hands and feet moved stiffly, petrified with fright. Well she might be frightened, face to face with the terrible things she had done. Her fault.

'They've all been assuming it must be a man,' he said, 'but suddenly I realised it didn't have to be.' They came to the pub. 'This is where I got the clue,' he explained. 'Could be a wumman, somebody said. And I thought - Well, I knew. Then it was all so clear. Everything fitted in. Every one of those murders – ' He paused. 'Even the very first one. It wasn't the boyfriend, it was you.'

'Matthew – ' she began to say.

He directed her towards the Moon and Stars. 'I drew up a chart. The proof is there. Every one of those murders happened when *I* wasn't with *you*.'

'No, Matthew,' she whispered, 'I wasn't with you.'

'Don't argue!' He slammed his fist on the dashboard and made her jump. The car juddered, but in the quiet Sunday-afternoon street there was no one to see. 'It was easy for you,' he said, 'with a car. Over the bridge. It didn't take long.' The black gap-toothed tenements rose above their heads. 'One of them happened just here. Somebody had followed her before, the papers said. Girls are afraid of that. Rape and murder, that's what they fear. You got her in the end.'

She licked her lips. Her voice was hoarse as sand. 'How am I supposed to have raped them, Matthew?' she said.

'With an instrument. Once with an old bit of piping from the car-park. Once with the handle of a wooden spoon.'

That shut her up. The gears screamed in another ham-fisted change. 'Do mind what you're doing, Louise,' he said. 'You see, it was quite possible. No alibi, and an instrument was used. You know about DNA.'

'Everybody does. You do.'

Matthew ignored her quibbling, because it was all proved in the cool columns of the chart. He saw it spread on the kitchen table, plotted out and clear. So much information; without the chart it would be impossible to hold in your mind. It danced before his eyes and he couldn't quite read it now, but it didn't matter. Through his body and nerves thrilled the knowledge of what Louise had done. He made her drive on and stop again on the bleak wasteground. Beside the Moon and Stars, where it began.

'One, two, three,' he said, laughing. There was a great freedom in speaking that out into the smoky air, under the flaming stalks of Dixon's Blazes. 'The One Two Three murders all happened just around here. There isn't necessarily a connection, that's what the police say. Between then and now. The One Two Three murders and now.' All those blonde girls. He shook his head to clear it as they melted together in his mind. 'But it's obvious to me. The same person killed them all. And it was you, Louise.'

'The same person?' she echoed, like somebody who wasn't very bright.

'Yes, yes.'

'In the 'sixties, in what was it, nineteen-sixty-eight, and now?'

'No doubt about it. No use denying it, Louise. It was you.'

'But Matthew, in nineteen-sixty-eight I was five years old.'

She hadn't said that.

'Then the night of the office party.' Full moon dodging behind veils of high thin cloud. Constant on the skyline, the tall chimneys, their roar and smoke and flame. The Moon and Stars squarely bright among the tenements, and a blonde girl walking home. 'That was here,' he said, 'just here.'

'The night of the office party?' said Louise.

He nodded. What happened that night, what happened on the other nights, rose in him like joy.

'The first of March? Six months after our wedding? In the alley?' she said.

'Remember it, do you?'

'Yes,' Louise said. 'And there wasn't a murder that night.'

'Feels as if there was,' he said. And then he saw Louise's face. 'What are you doing to me, Louise?' he yelled.

She was silent. He got a grip. Back to the chart, that so thoroughly proved her guilt. He saw the last line, the newly-added line. 'And now you've moved into the Merchant City,' he said. 'Spoiling it, spoiling our new life. Killing that blonde girl. Our downstairs neighbour. You shouldn't have done that, Louise.'

'Annelise Hansen? Nobody's killed her.'

He stared into her pudgy frightened face.

'I saw her today,' Louise said. 'Just as you were getting into the car. You saw her too.'

He looked into the abyss.

Louise leaned towards him. 'It's all right, Matthew. You see? You've done bad things but you didn't do that. And I – I'm going to leave work and look after you.' He saw the flicker in her eyes. She would promise anything, she was so frightened, anything at all.

She tuned into his doubt, he could tell. She started her stroking and coaxing again. It worked for him and it must have worked for her. Turned her on. Danger, great danger: that's what turns her on.

'I'll be with you,' she crooned. 'Looking after you. All the time. Just like Margaret. And nothing happened – 'The little glance into his face. The push into danger, saying what mustn't be said. The thrill. 'You didn't kill anybody,' she dared to say, 'while you were married to Margaret.'

'Well, only one or two,' he said.

That stopped her dead. She didn't know that, she realised. Margaret didn't tell her.

Well, Margaret didn't know.

Margaret stood in their warm red south-side living-room, looking at him while the evening paper screamed its headline news. Margaret did know. She couldn't admit it to Louise. Couldn't admit it to him. Couldn't admit it to herself.

She stood before him in her old skirt and cardigan. Apple-blossom scent. 'The migraine's gone now,' she said.

'It might have been three,' he said. 'Or four. Or five.'

Absolutely no colour in Louise's face. She tried to speak but she couldn't. Like Margaret in the last hospital bed.

'You should have told me,' Margaret said. Stern like his mother. As if it was his fault. When it was hers all along. Theirs. He punched out at Margaret, or his mother, or the girls in the back court, or Louise.

The day was nearly gone. He had lost an hour or two. It was sunset light he ran through, making for the bridge. Clear light, tinged with red. Behind him lay the terrible car.

Behind him lay the wasteground. He had chosen it as a bare place with no memories, but he carried them with him now. Behind him lay the south side, but that was with him too.

Tenements rose up beside Matthew as he ran. They were long gone, he knew that in the undeceiving light, but still he moved among them, looking for girls who called out to be killed. Short skirts. Their fault. One, two, three. Maybe five.

He ran under heavy south-side trees, though he knew they, like the tenements, weren't there. Girls moving among them too, though they weren't so clear in his mind. Not so many, only now and then. Afterwards he had gone home to Margaret, always there for him and safe. She coaxed it all away.

Always there. Not there now.

Now there's Louise. No, not now. The fearful car, cramped to screaming-point with her heavy lifeless body slumped across the front seats. The fogged windows and the smell.

Her fault. Her fault. Matthew reached the bridge and held himself upright by the scrolls and notches of its iron parapet. Must have been her fault. The river and the tenements spun round him and a long scarlet cloud had covered the sun. Back through the years: their fault, their fault. The girls in the back court and what his mother did to him.

His mother stood before him, blocking his path. Always watching him, asking questions, noticing what he was doing. Not knowing what he really wanted to do. He was free now and at last he did it, screaming his hate aloud.

An arm-linked boy and girl, just coming on to the bridge, stared, grey as the river, turned and ran. Matthew saw the boy fumble a mobile phone out of his pocket and clap it to his ear.

The dying sun dipped below its cloud and he saw that it wasn't his mother on the bridge at his feet. It was a wifie in a headscarf, her shopping-bag spilling tea-bags and baked beans. No, it was Margaret in her shroud.

'Stay with me,' he begged.

'It's your fault,' she said, crumbling into grey and white ash, blowing away on the river wind.

Louise stood before him with her swollen purple face. 'Your fault,' she said. 'Pulled down long ago. Nineteen fifty-nine or some damn year.'

He had heard her say it then. He heard it now. 'But they were there. I saw them,' he said.

He saw the chimneys, the ironworks, Dixon's Blazes, in the swinging sixties when he was young. Beyond the Moon and Stars, flame and smoke behind the blonde heads of young doomed girls. One, two, three, and Dixon's Blazes, blazing in his mind.

Pulled down long ago. Even then they were ten years gone. The smoke and flame, they can't have been there. They weren't there.

What else do I remember that wasn't there?

The river, the tenements, the bridge tilted under a scarlet sky. He didn't know what was false and what was true. His mother. What she did to him, and why. The girls in the back court? Did that ever happen at all? The blonde girls in the old black street? Everything shifted and he didn't know.

There are girls dead. One, two, three. Many more. That's true.

Louise is dead. That's true.

I killed her. That's very true.

He looked closely at the bridge he stood on. In its wrought-iron parapet you could find places to wedge a foot, secure a handhold, pull yourself high. Up there, sharp rusty metal scouring and gouging his palms, he looked down into the lazy water, slapping and sucking at the piers, rolling dark and deep away. Between his shoulder-blades Margaret's motherly hand pressed firm.